funeral
potatoes

funeral
potatoes

a novel

Joni Hilton

Covenant Communications, Inc.

Cover image © Jennifer Eichelberger, *Balancing Act.*

Cover design copyright © 2012 by Covenant Communications, Inc.

Published by Covenant Communications, Inc.
American Fork, Utah

Printed in the United States of America
First Printing: February 2012

18 17 16 15 14 13 12   10 9 8 7 6 5 4 3 2 1

ISBN-13: 978-1-60861-920-7

Dedicated to Bob, Richie, Brandon, Cassidy, and Nicole,
for being my travel companions through a life filled
with more material than I ever expected.
You're the best.

Acknowledgments

MANY PEOPLE ARE TO BE thanked for their contributions to this story. I'm grateful to Kathy Jenkins at Covenant Communications for her masterful editing and insights about this story.

While it is a work of fiction, there are chunks of outright truth in it as well.

Elda Hanks Boice Ekins was my visiting teacher before she passed away, and hers is the Ruby Barnes funeral where everyone who knew her through a dozen different ways she had touched them stood in recognition of her contribution to their lives. Elda was a go-getter and a great example of community involvement. In fact, I wrote a script for *Music and the Spoken Word* about her. We could use a thousand Elda Ekins!

These stories are also entirely true:

Praying for a loved one to have an accident happen that will shake them up and get them on the right path happened to one of my sons. Yes, he broke his collarbone in the crash, and yes, I apologized in the hospital.

French-speaking gorillas storming the California state capitol happened to my son, Brandon. He also came up with the hit-man plan, should he ever get Alzheimer's. And he is completely responsible for bringing three screaming geese to our house.

I owe the "butt bra" and wardrobe comments to my daughter, Nicole. She also experienced the monk and the steelhead trout stories.

The faked mission-call prank originated with my husband, Bob.

The math wizardry stories are all about our eldest son, Richie.

Our third son, Cassidy, took an aptitude test that told him to be a clown. You think such things aren't inherited? My husband, Bob, was a TV cartoon clown when he was fourteen.

The hidden Coca-Cola story came from my friend, Julie Pratt.

The chopped liver and fudge story came from my friend, Eleanor Coskey.

Cori Hucks, Deann Berns, and Monique Davis are the pals who came to my rescue during girls' camp, and Michelle Sterri is the darling Mia Maid with whom I shared my love of spas. Peanut the dog is named after a dachshund owned by Cori, and Syd's husband has the male form of Cori's name.

Alphabetically naming ridiculous things you're thankful for over your Thanksgiving feast was originated by Nicole, but is still carried on to this day by all four of our children.

The slippers worn to the ice cream parlor, the summons to the principal's office, the painted front door, all the crazy dog stories, the dream resulting in whiplash, the frog prevention call, the rest home incident, the Hawaiian visor gadget, the frozen yogurt excursion, the driver's license photo, the inability to grasp piano, the lack of hand-to-eye coordination, the bipolar handyman, the spinning class, and the girls' camp stories all happened to me. And, okay, sometimes I also drive like Cruella de Vil. And now you know why I write comedy.

Chapter 1

I AM COMPLETELY AGAINST FUNERALS. Death you cannot escape, but funerals are entirely optional. Here's what's wrong with them, in order:

1. They go on too long. An hour is plenty of time to recall a person's high points and to remind everyone about the plan of salvation. Having more than five speakers is ridiculous.
2. They require long drives to cemeteries, where all the women's high heels get stuck in the lawn.
3. They usually feature warbly singers. Let's be honest.
4. Children find viewings creepy. And so do I.
5. They require lavish, expensive floral arrangements that are then dragged to the cemetery, where they promptly wilt in the weather—wasting money that could have been put toward grandchildren's educations. I'm just saying.
6. People don't dress appropriately for them anymore. Oh, sure, a few folks wear black, but more and more you see tattered jeans and scruffy hair, as if this final tribute were no more important than running to the hardware store in the middle of painting a bathroom.

Now, I will grant you that the gathering of relatives and lifelong (deathlong?) friends can be a good thing, but why can't we just have a party? Why must we stare at the iffy makeup job on the poor fellow in the coffin? Why must we listen to speakers droning on until we wonder if going to funerals could cause strokes in and of itself, and thereby result in more deaths? Why must we analyze funeral sprays of tightly budded gladiola spears and wonder if they're going to get the chance to bloom? Why must we worry that the pallbearers are going to drop the casket? Don't we have enough on our minds with the passing of a loved one? Why do we have to deal with all these *arrangements?*

So back to my party idea. Some cultures do indeed have a wake, where folks simply get together to laugh and reminisce, to share great food and great memories. Isn't that what we all want our loved ones to do? And it would cost a lot less than most funerals, which usually include a luncheon afterward anyway.

I want mine to be a party-hats-and-confetti affair. No crying, no whining—only celebrating. I plan to hit the veil running and joyously burst onto a scene of dead relatives who are nudging each other and whispering, "Look out—she's back." I hope my sleeves will already be rolled up, because I plan to buckle down and work the second I get there, probably on genealogy records or missionary work. Will I stop to eat? Absolutely, and I expect truly heavenly meals. Will I enjoy the occasional massage? Of course! How else are the zillions of ministering angels going to occupy their eternity, if not cooking and catering?

Which brings me to funeral potatoes. This is the one vestige of funerals that we should keep because it's too traditional to LDS culture to abandon. That's not all: it will please me to know that those I've left behind are packing on the calories. Every American Mormon I know likes funeral potatoes, even the snobby foodies who cringe at the pounds of oil oozing out of the cheese and sliding all over the plate with the sour cream. Say what you will, this is our culture's comfort food, and we are glued together with the dairy products dripping from every bite.

So let the festivities begin, and let them begin with this recipe, which you are to memorize, lest you be kidnapped someday and your only chance for freedom is to win the hearts of your captors with a recipe that will leave them weak and groaning:

FUNERAL POTATOES
2 10.75-oz. cans cream of chicken soup
2 C. sour cream
2 C. grated cheddar cheese
½ C. chopped onion
½ C. butter, melted
1 32-oz. bag frozen Southern-style (not shredded) hash browns, thawed
Topping:
2 C. finely crushed corn flakes
2 T. butter, melted

Preheat oven to 350 degrees. Grease a 9 x 13-inch baking dish. In a large bowl, stir soups, sour cream, cheese, onions, and the ½ C. melted butter. Fold in hash browns. Pour mixture into pan. Combine crushed corn flakes and butter; sprinkle on top. Bake for 30 minutes.

There are dozens of variations—add crumbled, cooked bacon, or use Gouda instead of cheddar, for example—but they are blasphemous and should be avoided. Thou shalt not mess with an existing recipe that everyone likes. (I personally could add a number of commandments to the list you already know, and that would be a good place to start.)

Incidentally, a good fridge magnet for you to paint at your next Relief Society activity is this: FAT PEOPLE ARE HARDER TO KIDNAP. And it's got to be true, right? I mean, think about a crew of guys trying to get a gigantic burlap sack around a tubby victim, and then dragging that person out of there—nearly impossible. I'm just saying.

So now you have your marching instructions if I should kick the bucket anytime soon. Party. Potatoes. People.

I guess I haven't said much about the people yet. I want everyone there, of course. There are far too many cousins who don't even know each other, and I think every death should launch a spontaneous family reunion. I mean *something* good ought to come of it, right?

Allow me to introduce the main cast of characters who had better show up at my funeral . . . I mean, my *party*.

Let's start at the bottom of the heap. My brother Ted is the family ne'er-do-well. If you don't have a ne'er-do-well in your family, you are probably lying and could possibly be the ne'er-do-well yourself.

For those of you who've never heard the term, a *ne'er-do-well* is a lazy, irresponsible person who is sometimes described as worthless or good for nothing. But I think those descriptions are a bit harsh, or at least a bit outside the gospel idea that there's hope for everyone. Sure, perhaps Ted has "never done well" in his life, but that doesn't mean he never will, right? Call me naïve, but I still believe Ted will grow up one day, stop drinking beer just to fry my mother, stop fishing on Sundays just to fry my dad, and admit that we're all on to something pretty exciting with the restored gospel of Jesus Christ. I have hope that he will stop dodging his home teachers, find and marry a wonderful woman in the temple, and become the family patriarch that we'll all look up to once Mom and Dad have their final going-away parties.

Ted is the oldest, in his early forties, and still hasn't had a steady relationship or a steady job for more than six months at a time. He looks like one of those tycoons who retired at thirty-five and let his hair grow long, minus the tycoon part. He wears sleeveless parkas and an occasional mustache, and has sandy blond hair that looks intentionally messy. If someone told you he was in a rock band, you'd believe it. He lives in a trailer with an Irish setter named Hooligan and makes lamps out of odd objects that he sells to tourists in beach towns where they lose their judgment just long enough to think an oil can would make a cool lamp for their family room and they take it home to Omaha.

I estimate that Ted has supplied approximately six percent of all garage sale items across America.

We invite Ted over for dinner every Monday night; he always accepts and always enjoys the meal. Then I invite him to stay for family home evening, at which point he always has something more pressing to do. But he's polite and loves my kids, which earns him an eternity of weekly dinners as far as I'm concerned. He comes to their plays and ball games, and once I almost got him to a baptism. But he always stops short of coming to church or delving into a serious talk about it. Unless, of course, it's a funeral. He does attend those, because, well, it's just too disrespectful not to.

My husband, Cory, thinks Ted's behavior is one elongated rebellion against the "OverAchiever family," a moniker he gave the OllerVanKeefer family (my ponderous maiden name) shortly after he met us all. And he may be right. All the other siblings went on missions, finished college, earned advanced degrees, and/or stayed active in the Church and made our parents proud. Ted missed the boat. Ever since then he has been trying to prove he never wanted on in the first place.

The next sibling is my sister, Donna. Donna is the Scrapbook Queen. Oh, I know you think you already know a scrapbook queen, but trust me: Donna could keep a number of therapists busy with her obsession (all while making scrapbooks of their therapy sessions). And, yes, she probably has a separate charge card that her husband, Jerry, has no idea exists. What's that? Did I hear you gasp just now? Is it because you thought this sort of duplicity was a *secret*? Please. I've talked to the cashiers at the craft stores, and a huge percentage of their shoppers are women with separate charge accounts for their scrapbooking.

Donna's husband, Jerry, is a successful obstetrician who has delivered countless children, and Donna has scrapbooked nearly every one of them. In addition to keeping meticulous photographic records of her own five children, she also takes pictures of any of Jerry's patients who want in on her neurosis.

She does a whole presentation for them when they give birth, bestowing them with a book that documents their entire pregnancy with serrated scissors and embossing powder. Donna has added a whole wing to their already huge home that is dedicated entirely to this hobby. She has more paper than the *New York Times* and more Crickets than the early pioneers.

Born just after Ted, she raced through school at breakneck pace, making *two* posters for all her reports instead of the required *one*. Ted stumbled to the finish line in high school; Donna was right on his heels as valedictorian of her class. In college she completed a double major—graphic art and drama, both of which are evident as she bounds into the hospital rooms of new mothers, no flourish spared, and presents them with their "First Scrapbook," one that Donna thinks will inspire them to great heights in cutting and gluing but that will undoubtedly intimidate them and prevent them from ever attempting a similar effort.

Needless to say, many an observer has been utterly lost in the wake of Donna's speedboat, and Ted almost spun as she whizzed by. While he was still struggling to find himself, Donna served a mission to Norway and looked as if she might light the entire rest of the world on fire as well.

And, oh, the applause. Everywhere she went, Donna was dazzling. It wasn't just her fluffy head of blond curls, either. It was her energy. Teachers, classmates, and acquaintances of every kind all stood in awe of Donna. But what probably bothered Ted the most, as he was working on his prodigal son act, was that our parents were bursting with pride over this whirling dervish daughter. A virtual shrine to her accomplishments went up in the hallway. Ted had to pass the ribbons and awards every day, knowing he'd been outshined. More than once I heard him call it the "Hall of Shame."

Two more boys came along shortly after Donna—both athletic wonders who accomplished so much that Donna served as a motivator and cheerleader for them instead of being a threat. The first was Neal, whose high school principal singled him out during the graduation ceremony as the most outstanding student the school had ever had—an all-around great guy who excelled in both sports and academics and was so handsome he was voted Senior King. Neal was blushing as red as his cap and gown, and the rest of us were beaming. All except Ted, that is, who was chafing a bit as his younger brother joined Donna in the group of OllerVanKeefer champions.

Just as Neal was leaving for his mission to Italy, Chad stepped into the spotlight as a national debate champion and MVP of his high school's baseball team. I could almost read Ted's thoughts: *Will there be no end to the awards in that blasted hallway?*

Chad then served a mission to Ecuador. As Neal became a CPA, Chad became a lawyer. Both of them married in timely fashion and started darling little families of towheaded, blue-eyed children, all earning stars in kindergarten and keeping up the OllerVanKeefer name.

This is when I saw Ted finally soften. He stepped into the role of uncle to these kids as if it had been designed with him in mind. When their dads were busy working, Ted was the great big kid who took them to creeks where they could catch frogs or to a friend's ranch where they could ride horses. He played video games with them, taught them magic tricks, and took them camping, where they saw their first shooting stars. I often wished there could be Uncle Awards—Ted would need his own hallway.

And where do I fit into this lineup? I'm the baby, Sydney Rose, born just after Chad. I came into the world thirty-three years ago, just as Mom was turning forty and Dad was saying they were too old to have any more kids. But there I was: another OllerVanKeefer kid who shared the same relentless drive, blond hair, and freckled cheeks as all the others.

I followed the boys in sports, trying everything they did but finally settling on track. I loved the wind in my hair, the burn in my legs, and the great feeling of winning a race. The trophies began to accumulate, a scholarship followed, and soon I had graduated from college, married, and settled down with Cory, a wonderful guy I've known since high school. Cory has no interest whatsoever in track but can play any musical instrument you hand him.

By now Ted was thirty-two and at least mature enough to be cheering from the sidelines when I won a local marathon at twenty-three. He even snapped photos and laughingly said they were for "Mom and Dad's Hall of Fame."

Soon after that, Cory and I learned we were having a baby—and I found that while I wasn't running marathons, I was nevertheless running every which way as more children arrived. A morning run in the cool weather was plenty now; then I'd dig into my day, grateful for every minute (well, *almost* every minute) of watching my kids grow. Donna dutifully scrapbooked them, sure I would not do the job justice, and I was grateful to be off the hook on that one.

"You live a charmed life," Annie said to me in the kitchen over lunch one day. She's tall and curvy and reminds me of a gypsy. Annie and I worked together in Primary a couple of years ago and are still tight pals. She must have seen me raise my eyebrows. "You do, Syd," she said. "Your husband is the elders quorum president, you have a beautiful home, and your kids all get along."

I laughed. Okay, the first part was true; Cory *was* the elders quorum president. But our house was usually a shambles and my most frequent prayer was for help in teaching our kids to get along and love one another. We even have a jar filled with quarters from times we've caught the kids being rude or unkind to each other. I waved at the scene before her—the scattered toys and books, the basket of laundry waiting to go upstairs, and two of my kids tugging on an action figure until its head popped off. Vinyl lettering on nearly every spare wall of our home virtually bursts with quotes about love and kindness, my subtle—or not-so-subtle—attempt at subliminal parenting.

But Annie's husband was out of work, they were looking for a smaller home, and she had finally moved her two sons into separate rooms to keep them from killing each other.

"It's all relative," I said, bringing up a couple of sisters in the ward. "Look at Theresa. She'd love to have kids—any kind of kids. And Jen says she cries every night because she's not married. I mean, really, we're blessed."

Annie shook her head and took another bite of my spinach salad, the one I make with strawberries, avocados, and a blender dressing that includes Worcestershire sauce. "Trust you to be grateful."

I faked a remorseful face. "I am truly sorry," I said. "I need to repent of that."

"Not funny," she said. "Of course I'm grateful. I'm just jealous, too."

Now I laughed. "I don't think you can be both at the same time."

"Well, I'm doing it."

I handed her a second roll, ones I picked up at the farmers' market that morning as my kids were wailing and begging to get to the honey stand. Blackberry honey sticks were their favorite, and Cory loved buckwheat honey.

I popped the action figure's head back on and put it on top of the fridge, sent the kids to separate places to play for a while, then sat down again with Annie. Just then my cell phone rang and I picked it up while pouring each of us more lemonade. I listened, unblinking. I could feel my eyes turning glassy. Finally I thanked the caller, one of my cousins, and hung up.

"My favorite uncle just died," I said. "Uncle Dan."

Annie threw her arms around me. "I'm so sorry," she said. She smelled like night-blooming jasmine. "And I'm sorry for accusing you of having such a smooth life. I can be so short-sighted sometimes." She offered to babysit the kids, bring us a meal, make calls for me—all things I couldn't even process just yet. But her love came through and I thanked her for that. Annie left me to break the news to my kids and gave me another long hug at the front door.

"Call me for anything," she said. I nodded.

I made a call to Cory, who stepped out of a meeting and offered to come right home. I told him there was really nothing he could do, but he cut his day short anyway just to ease my schedule and help with the kids.

More calls poured in; I made a few myself then simply sat on a chair and cried. Ellie, my oldest, came and put her little arm around my shoulders. "I guess you'll be making more funeral potatoes," she said softly.

I laughed through the tears. I know she was trying to comfort me, trying to offer up wisdom from her little nine-year-old soul, but it sounded so dismal and somber, almost like a warning. *This looks like a call for* (drumroll here) *funeral potatoes.*

And who knows? Maybe that's how she sees my funeral potatoes—the sign of a grave event, the culinary form of an ambulance. It was definitely time to rally the troops and draw together as a family, and in our culture, the first thing you do is get out the pots and pans.

Chapter 2

BLACK DRESS, BLACK HEELS, BLACK PURSE. Ready. Oh—and funeral potatoes in a casserole carrier. Uncle Dan had been a temple worker and bishop and had served a mission to Minnesota with my Aunt Pauline years ago. Beloved by one and all, his funeral was a packed house.

As always, I found myself scanning the crowd for Ted, hoping he'd be sitting where he could hear some shred of the gospel plan that would be his turning point. I'd pray for some moment when he'd look around at the people, the building, even the benches, and think, "This is where I belong. Why have I been kidding myself?"

After dropping off the potatoes to the kitchen crew, Cory and I ushered our four kids to the pews. Ellie led the way with dramatic flair inherited from her Aunt Donna. She was followed by our sons, Hayden and Joshua, and finally little one-year-old Tootsie Pop—who, if we didn't start calling her Juliet, was going to have a permanent nickname as indelible as if we had written it on her forehead with a Sharpie®.

Cory and I positioned ourselves strategically between Hayden and Joshua (aka "The Usual Suspects") and hoped they'd behave themselves through the service. Hayden's cowlick wouldn't lay flat despite an extra coating of hair gel, and Joshua's clip-on tie was curling at the bottom from having been rolled into a tube and shoved into his pocket all week.

Just as the organ prelude music stopped and the funeral was about to begin, I saw Ted slip in at the back. He despises viewings as much as I do, and shows up just for the service. He also despises well-meaning relatives who wander aimlessly through the viewing room then waddle over to ask him if he has a job or a girlfriend yet.

I have to say that as funerals go, this one was about as good as it gets. Aunt Pauline had died six years ago, so everyone was rejoicing that she and Uncle Dan were now reunited. Funny stories were told (including Uncle Dan's penchant for acquiring traffic tickets while racing to discount movie showings) and the restored gospel was explained in its simple, yet glorious, perfection.

My parents, now seventy-six and seventy-three, were squeezing each other's hands and smiling through their tears.

"How can anybody hear this and not want to sign right up?" I whispered to Cory.

"He's listening," he said, knowing exactly what I was thinking.

My cousins, who were weeping openly for the loss of their wonderful dad, had asked the oldest one to speak. It took Rick a few minutes to compose himself, and then he said something that thunders through me with the magnitude of truth every time I hear it.

"Nothing has happened here that is of eternal consequence," he said. Then he repeated it. And then, for those there who were not of our faith—and there were many—he explained.

"My parents were sealed for eternity and filled their lives with service to God," he said. "Their place in the eternities is certain. They have simply moved on to a different venue—a better, happier one. When death comes to a righteous servant of God, there is no tragedy, only joy in knowing they've gone home to a grand reunion."

Then he talked about the premortal existence, eternal families, and the hereafter.

"The real tragedies in life are those who turn away from God, who head down paths of sin or carelessness. Those are the ones we should mourn today, but definitely not my dad."

And then I lost it. I thought of Ted, the tragedy he was living, and my shoulders shook as I struggled to contain the tears streaming down my face. Suddenly I was grateful he was sitting far behind me and couldn't read my thoughts the way he could if he were close by. Cory reached behind Joshua and rubbed my neck.

I took a huge breath and exhaled, willing the tears to stop. How long had I been praying that we'd all be together in the temple one day? Since I was a teenager, some twenty years ago? Longer? I mentally sought scriptures about people who'd waited much longer than that for their prayers to be answered as I tried to fight off the self-pity.

I thought of Annie, who was jealous of my life. She had no such anguish in hers—*she* was the person with an easy life if you think about things from an eternal perspective. Financial trouble, kids who quarrel—these pale in comparison to spiritual death and separation from God.

The funeral ended, and, as everyone filed out, I kept my eyes down. I was afraid to see Ted—afraid I'd burst into tears. Or slug him. I wasn't sure which. Cory held me in the foyer for a moment and whispered, "All in the Lord's time," which oddly made me madder. I regret hissing back into his ear, "Ted's losing his window of opportunity to have a wife and children!" At that point various family members cut me off (a good thing) by coming up to share how beautiful the funeral was. And it was. Rick's comments were perfect. And so true. I think Cory was relieved that all these relatives were sidetracking my tangent. And once I calmed down, I suppose they saved me from getting worked into a lather that wouldn't have served any constructive purpose and that definitely would have been the wrong way to greet Ted a few minutes later.

The sun was glaring off the limousines as we crept through traffic to the rolling green cemetery, where a touching graveside service left us all understandably weepy. Then we headed back to the bustling meetinghouse for the luncheon. Like another comforting hug, there was the familiar lineup of sliced ham, green Jell-O salad, dinner rolls, and funeral potatoes. Five or six pans of them, looking just like mine, were waiting in the kitchen for helpful deacons to bring each one out when the previous pan was emptied.

"I waited until yours was brought out." It was Ted, sitting down with us, paper plate in hand, winking as he took a bite of my dish.

I smiled. "How did you know which one was mine?"

"The Pyrex dish with masking tape burned on one end." He shrugged. It was true—my mom had brought brownies to us in it once, and when one of the kids mentioned the burned-on tape, she had decided to leave the pan with me. Evidently she had taken it to a ward dinner some months before, filled with a noodle casserole and carefully labeled with "OllerVanKeefer" written on some tape, and someone had put it in the oven to warm it up. The tape burned on permanently, and she had never liked it since. But I, the most handed-down-to family member, was happy to get an extra Pyrex dish, and have gladly used it ever since.

"So how did you like the service?" Cory asked him.

"Perfect," Ted said. "Really captured Uncle Dan. Of course, you can't tell all the stories; there'd never be time."

"I like the one about the snake," Hayden said. (Is there a family in the country who does not have at least half a dozen good snake stories?) The one Hayden likes—but that went untold at the funeral—is the one about when Uncle Dan and Aunt Pauline went camping with their ward high priests quorum some thirty years ago. Uncle Dan had to get up in the night to use the restroom, which was situated about a hundred yards away. On the way back he spotted a harmless kingsnake, coiled up, asleep on a tarp. He grabbed it and thought he'd play a trick on Aunt Pauline. So he tossed it into their tent then stood back and waited for her to scream.

Oh, there was a scream, all right. Uncle Dan had gotten the wrong tent. The stake president's wife flew out in her underwear, eyes white as cue balls, hair standing on end, and was soon joined by everyone else in camp—they all thought a bear must have attacked someone. Her husband quickly threw the snake out of the tent, crawled out himself, and covered his wife with a blanket.

Evidently there stood Uncle Dan, right by the tent door, as if he were a Minute Man or something—the hero who was first on the scene to rescue poor Sister Davies. Everyone began patting him on the back. Sister Davies herself even said, "Oh, my gracious! Thank you, Dan, for coming to my rescue." Uncle Dan gulped and never admitted his mistake until years later at a stake barbecue, at which point Aunt Pauline promptly slapped him in the face.

"That wasn't for trying to scare me with a snake," she said. "It was for making Sister Davies run out of her tent in her underwear."

Word got back to Sister Davies, but by now she was able to laugh about it. "I think he's had enough years of tortured conscience," she said.

The snake story ended up on the cutting-room floor and didn't make it into the funeral speeches. But another favorite one did—the story of Uncle Dan's moment in the sun as European royalty. Years ago he and Aunt Pauline went to Germany for the famous Oberammergau passion play about Christ that's performed every ten years.

As they were checking in at their hotel, the nearsighted clerk ran their credit card and then breathlessly asked, "Your last name is Oberammergau?" And then, like a "Who's on First" bit from Abbot and Costello, Uncle Dan—whose hearing was not all it could be—thought the fellow said, "OllerVanKeefer" with a German accent. So he responded in his best German, "Ja, das ist mein name." Aunt Pauline, who always thought people were kidding when they weren't, simply laughed and nodded.

Well, as you might expect, rumors went flying. The hotel upgraded them to a lavish presidential suite, baskets of fruit and flowers began arriving, and faxes came pouring in with hopes that Uncle Dan would be pleased with the upcoming performance. A special limousine was dispatched to bring them to the event, where they were seated as VIPs and wildly applauded and bowed to, as if they were the German chancellor and his wife.

Meanwhile, Uncle Dan had no clue this was all due to a misunderstanding; he just thought the Germans were genuinely pleased to have American tourists. The Germans repeatedly said how great an honor it was to have them there, and Uncle Dan obliged by nodding and smiling and shaking as many hands as were extended to him. Aunt Pauline was the gracious, smiling temple worker she always was, her eyes twinkling as she greeted fan after fan.

This went on for about four days—complimentary gourmet meals, free massages, the works—until another hotel worker looked at the registration more carefully and probably said, "It says 'OllerVanKeefer,' you dummkopf!" We can all imagine him smacking the first clerk upside the head.

Suddenly the star treatment came to a screeching halt. Officious chamber maids came in, snatched away the bouquets and fruit baskets, and glared at Uncle Dan and Aunt Pauline. Tight-lipped bellboys escorted them out onto the street muttering something about "Hochstaplers," which Uncle Dan did not know meant *imposters* but thought was Aunt Pauline's maiden name, Hochsteader. So while Uncle Dan was trying to find out why Hochsteaders were not welcome at the hotel, the staff was alarmed that he was pointing to his wife and joining the accusation that she was an imposter.

A pair of policemen happened by just then, and the hotel manager decided this might, indeed, be a fraud worth pursuing. So while Uncle Dan and Aunt Pauline stood there on the street with their luggage, the hotel manager explained his entire grievance to the authorities. Now the police turned to Uncle Dan and, in a stroke of luck that probably saved my aunt and uncle from landing in the clink, one of the cops spoke excellent English.

Slowly the evil scheme of the conspiring Americans unraveled into the innocent goof of a desk clerk, and my relatives were released with profuse apologies and tremendous embarrassment by the hotel manager. Whether they're still laughing over it in Germany we will never know, but it certainly brings chuckles on this side of the Atlantic every time a family member tells the tale.

Another story that was shared was about the time Uncle Dan played a trick on a kid in his ward who had just been called on a mission. He and Evan Stichmanovich had become close buddies, and Evan had told Uncle Dan that he wanted him to be on hand when he received his mission call and opened the letter. As soon as the envelope arrived, Sister Stichmanovich called Uncle Dan and invited him over.

"Is Evan there?" Uncle Dan asked.

"No, he's on his way home from work."

"So he hasn't seen the envelope yet?"

"No, why?"

There was no time to explain. Uncle Dan got busy on the computer and typed up a fake mission call, stuck it in a regular envelope, and dashed over to the Stichmanovich's house.

They all gathered around for the big moment, and Evan nervously tore open Uncle Dan's letter. "Dear Elder Stichmanovich," he read, "You have been called to the Lebanon Baghdad Mission, Farsi sign language speaking." Evan gulped, then continued. "You will need to change your name to Smith because Stichmanovich is much too long for sign language and too difficult to pronounce for everyone else."

By now everyone was laughing and Evan finally realized—with huge relief—that Uncle Dan was up to his old tricks. He glanced at the bottom of the fake letter and saw the characteristic signature, "Dan the Man."

Then the real letter was produced, and everyone cheered as Evan learned he would be serving in Lubbock, Texas, English speaking. But he saved Uncle Dan's letter and read it at his farewell—and it reappeared today at the funeral, eliciting laughter all over again.

I looked across the table at Ted. *This is your family,* I wanted to say. *These are your stories. These are the people you're sealed to. You need to come back.*

He caught my eye and smiled. And I vowed not to die before seeing that same smile in the temple, however long it might take.

Chapter 3

DID I MENTION THAT WE own an utterly lawless Chihuahua? While we were all at Uncle Dan's funeral, this rat-in-a-dog-suit was shredding the throw pillows I had just bought, overpriced but so perfect I bought them anyway. We came home to a living room filled with so much downy fluff it looked like a blizzard had come in through an open window. Not likely, since we live in Sacramento.

Of course the kids were overjoyed. Cory was "scolding" little Peanut in his gentle teaching voice that sounds like praise if I ever heard it, and I was so livid my neck was turning purple. "Give me one reason why we keep that dog alive," I muttered as I rounded up some trash bags. Our other dog—Freckles, the chubby pointer on a senior kibble diet—was snoozing right where we'd left him on his red plaid bed in the family room. Cory and I got him just after we were married, and he was always the picture of obedience. Perfect and housebroken from the beginning, Freckles was the ideal family companion. In fact, he was plenty. But Cory is wrapped around all ten of Ellie's fingers, and when she wanted to visit the pound "just to look at the puppies," any dope could have predicted the outcome: A newly adopted terror in the form of a wet nose and a wagging tale.

Ellie was dancing through the pillow fluff. "Let's leave it until Christmas," she pleaded. "It can be the snow!" And thus we see, to borrow a phrase from Mormon, why children should not be allowed to make household decisions.

On top of this search-and-destroy gene, the dog is incorrigible. This means she cannot be taught, cannot learn, and is an idiot of a dog. We have crated her from day one, read and applied every dog training technique known to man, and still she is not housebroken. You've heard of the Dog Whisperer? I am on the brink of having my own reality show called the Dog Murderer.

"Oh, you know you love her." Ellie was gushing as she held the quivering little criminal in her arms. "Doesn't she wuv you? Doesn't she wuv you?" she said, nuzzling the beast's neck. Peanut looked up at me with those brown marble eyes, posing like a pitiful waif, despite a brain the size of a grape.

Ellie turned to me. "Don't you love Peanut?"

I sighed. "I love peanut butter," I said. "How about we make her into that?"

Two hours later I had just vacuumed up the last bits of destruction when the Carltons rang the doorbell. Peanut now launched into yet another of her choice talents: yapping. Will someone please explain to me why dogs never get laryngitis? Mercifully, Hayden scooped her up and kept her from clawing the paint off the door, which I then opened.

"Are we too early?" they asked, a pie in hand.

I had completely forgotten that we had invited Eric and Liza Carlton over for dinner. They're members of our old ward who had no idea we had just been to a funeral—let alone that we had just cleaned up after a one-dog demolition crew.

"No, come in, come in," I said, my mind scouring mental images of the fridge and freezer contents.

"Oh, Syd, we caught you off guard," Liza said, reading the panic on my face. Liza and Eric are the bubbly, fun folks welcome at every party, beautifully able to laugh at themselves, and dear friends who I knew would forgive my lapse in planning. Eric is bald and chubby, and Liza has a full head of lustrous auburn hair, usually flowing at her shoulders but swept into a stylish chignon tonight. She cooks like a French chef (hence Eric's expanding waistline) and runs a dinner co-op for her extremely fortunate neighbors.

Cory stepped in and explained, and I interrupted to assure them we could still have dinner. My mind had long ago abandoned images of the fridge and freezer contents and was now mentally scanning take-out menus in the junk drawer.

"We can come back another time," they said, but my kids were already eyeing the pie. I must admit my memory of Liza's pie-making skills was still sharp as ever, so I took the pie and led her and Eric into the kitchen.

"I'll go get Chinese," Cory offered, and I assured the Carltons we could throw together a salad to enjoy until he got back. Ellie helped snap Juliet into her high chair as the boys distributed napkins and I began cutting up lettuce and tomatoes.

The kids, of course, regaled the Carltons with funeral stories, and when Cory got back we dished up the chow mein, fried rice, and lemon chicken. Then Liza shared a funeral story of their own. Liza's grandmother had passed away in Salt Lake City a few months earlier, and one of her uncles eulogized her by sharing a secret. The grandmother had loved Coca-Cola®. When her husband became bishop, he declared, "No more Coke in the house." Well, it turns out the grandmother had had a credit card at Castleton's for *years* that her husband had known nothing about (what did I tell you?), so something as easy as hiding Coke was child's play for her. There was an old-fashioned milk can in the kitchen for recycled newspapers, mail, ads, and other discarded paper. The kids knew that only the top two-thirds was paper. The bottom third was where their mother hid her cans of Coke.

We all laughed, and Liza said, "Oh, wait. That was just the secondary stash. She kept the cold stuff in the toilet tank."

Hayden jumped up and pretended to be dashing off to check the toilet tanks, but Cory caught him by the collar and sat him down again. "Trust me," he said, "if your mom is addicted to anything, it's running—and I don't think you can hide that in a toilet tank."

"I don't know," Liza said. "Ours is always running."

We groaned at her joke, and I confessed that my morning run was getting shorter and shorter all the time. I still enjoyed it but had so many other priorities that I always seemed to be choosing best over better.

"Like sleeping in," Cory said. "Nah, I'm kidding. I know it's reading scriptures with the kids."

The Carltons' kids were all in their teens and twenties now, and Liza was my role model; I took careful notes as her kids entered each stage before mine did. I asked how the kids were doing.

"Oh, trust me," she said. "If you have a teenage daughter you do not also need a mirror." Then she told us that the other day she had been standing in the bathroom in only her underwear, leaning in to the mirror to put on her makeup. She saw her thirteen-year-old daughter walk in and stand there watching her for a few minutes.

Liza said, "I was thinking, *How nice. This is so sweet—my daughter is probably thinking how she'll wear makeup someday, and she's seeing how I do it.* But no. After a minute or so she asked, 'Mom, do they make a butt bra?'"

We all burst out laughing. "I kid you not," Liza said. "That's what she was staring at—*not* my face."

"Hey, gravity gets us all," Eric said.

"Nothing like offspring to keep you humble," Cory laughed.

Liza nodded. "And some are a little more 'off' than others." Then she told us how her entire closet has been pillaged and plundered by her seventeen-year-old daughter, Chloe, who simultaneously criticizes everything Liza chooses to wear. "She makes up careers for me based on what I'm wearing," Liza said. "Did you know that I was the ambassador from Nairobi? Well, according to Chloe I am." Chloe thinks a certain brown pantsuit of Liza's looks exactly like something the Nairobi ambassador might wear. She has also tagged a pink blouse "the secretary to the Dean of Anthropology top," a pair of running pants "the Soul Train pants," and a tan tunic with gold trim is dubbed a costume from a Hebrew play. A lavender pullover is the "I Give Up" top, and an autumn sweater adorned with seasonal motifs is the "Why Not Just Wear a Sign That Says I'm a Felt Board" sweater.

At that point we were all laughing, and I recalled the last time I went shopping with my nieces—Donna's daughters—and one of them told me I was too old to buy a silver handbag, but that bronze would be okay. Another one took some sunglasses out of my hands and said, "Oh, you don't want those, Aunt Syd—those are wangster."

"What is *wangster*?" I asked.

"It's when white people try to do gangster bling. It's called Wangster."

So I can't have anything sparkly? Sheesh—and kids think *we* have a lot of rules!

"Last week," Liza said, "I got a call from the principal at Chloe's high school. He wanted to see me about Chloe signing permission slips with my name. Eric and I had gone to England for that week, remember? So I had told her she could sign my name on whatever came up. It's not like it's illegal, right?"

We were all listening, nodding.

"Okay, it turns out it *is* illegal," Liza said. Liza was summoned to the principal's office so he could explain the rules about this and so she could sign another paper to verify the difference in handwriting. That afternoon, Liza picked Chloe up from school and said, "Guess what—I had to go to the principal's office today."

Chloe whipped around, aghast, and said, "In *those* pants?"

Now, in *my* day if someone had been summoned by the principal it was cause for shock and gasping: Not the *principal*! What did you *do*?

But that was Chloe's last concern. Her major worry was that her mother had been seen wearing her Soul Train pants. I tell you, it's enough to make you want to go home and put on your "I Give Up" top.

By now my cheeks were hurting from the laughter, and we all decided it was high time we enjoyed Liza's peaches-and-cream pie. The kids, of course, also wanted to crack open their fortune cookies.

Here is why Mormons do not put a lot of stock in fortune cookies. Okay, first and most obvious is that some guy scribbling out his thoughts in a cookie factory cannot possibly predict your future. Second, this is a poor substitute for a real dessert. And third, fortune cookies tend to be, well, stupid.

They don't even tell your fortune anymore. Most of them give you advice, and lousy advice at that. "Always listen before you speak." Ridiculous, right? People don't listen before they speak. We just speak up, say what's on our minds, and blabber away. It's more fun.

"Dare to drean." One time mine honestly said this—just as you read it, with an *n* instead of an *m*. I have been dreaning ever since, and nothing has improved. Clearly there is no final editor approving the copy in a Chinese fortune cookie plant.

"A wise man remembers the past." But he doesn't bring it up in every argument or he'll drive his wife crazy.

"Your first idea is the best one." No, my first idea is always the worst one, such as the night I decided to strangle the cat next door who keeps howling every night. Five or six days later I finally bought a sound machine. Now, wasn't that a better choice?

Hayden read his fortune to us. "Try to avoid fat igloos."

Ah. Sage advice. Cory looked over his shoulder. "It says 'Try to avoid fatigue.'" An easy mistake any young reader could make.

Actually, I think avoiding fat igloos is also a good idea, as it would mean you have ventured into an inhospitable climate, and should turn around and go back.

Some enterprising member of the Church should market LDS fortune cookies. We could serve them for refreshments along with our famous red punch. Can't you just imagine the reactions?

"You will have to pay for all your children's weddings, even the boys'."

"Your home teaching families will never let you in."

"There are weevils in your wheat."

"You will soon give a talk in sacrament meeting."

"You will be the next bishop."

"Your child is the biggest brat in Primary."

Hilarious.

My cookie actually contained a fortune instead of advice this time. "Your toilets will be recognized," it said.

Again, Cory took the fortune and shook his head. "Your eyes are going bad." He laughed. "It says your *talents* will be recognized."

Oh, well. At least it was an actual fortune. But to think my toilets will now have to live in anonymity. Such is life. I should've hidden Cokes in them.

Then, of course, the conversation wound back around to death, and Eric Carlton said he had just taken out a life insurance policy on himself in case he should he die before Liza does. Our kids were too young to have ever heard of life insurance policies, so Cory explained it. (Being an attorney, Cory's explanations can be a bit, shall we say, lengthy.)

"Do you have one?" Ellie asked her dad.

"Of course," Cory said. "If I should die before your mom—but I don't think that'll be until I'm ninety-three or so—she'll get a million dollars."

"What?!" Hayden exclaimed, once again only partially paying attention. "If you die, Mom will get ninety-three million dollars?"

Cory rolled his eyes.

"Are you kidding?" I said to Hayden. "Do you think if that man was worth ninety-three million dollars he'd be sitting there right now?"

As everybody burst out laughing, Cory looked at me with mock gratitude. I grinned back at him and shrugged. "I'm just saying," I said.

We both cleared the few dishes there were then he hugged me by the sink. "Can't say as I'd blame you." He laughed. "I'd do the same thing."

I swatted him with a towel. "Thanks a lot."

When we got back to the table, the kids were talking about what would happen to them if we died.

"Oh, your parents probably have that all worked out in their wills," Eric was saying.

Cory and I glanced at each other; we had never even discussed it. And, of course, this was not something up for debate, but that has never stopped our children from wildly campaigning for their causes. I was sure they'd argue over whether Aunt Donna, Uncle Neal, or Uncle Chad should raise them, but to my surprise they all wanted Uncle Ted.

"He's the most fun," Joshua said.

I couldn't help smiling to realize how much they loved him. I would have picked one of the others, especially one who had a gospel-centered home with church and seminary attendance a big priority. But the kids were too young to think about those things. They were simply choosing their favorite uncle.

Cory squeezed my hand. "Mom and I will have to take care of that," he said, clearly as surprised as I was. "Meanwhile, you kids don't need to worry—I think you'll have us around long after you're grown and have kids of your own."

"Eww," Ellie said. "You'll be a grandpa and a grandma."

I nodded. "Yep. But we'll still be cool." I think Cory and I are the only ones who believe that.

That conversation was still on my mind that night as we were getting ready for bed, and I realized that if Ted somehow did end up being their guardian, maybe it would reactivate him—he'd have to agree to daily scripture study and prayer, family home evening, the whole package. And with startling clarity, I realized it would actually be worth it if it brought him back. Physical death would be a small price to pay for spiritual rebirth and the knowledge that our family truly would be together forever, no empty chairs, no missing brothers.

Chapter 4

THE NEXT SATURDAY DONNA ASKED me to come over and help her with a massive project she was doing for the young women in her ward. As their new president, she decided each of them should have a fluffy down pillow top for her mattress to remind her that she is the daughter of royalty, a princess at night as well as during the day. And, of course, *buying* mattresses toppers was out of the question. These pillow-top flying carpets must be *handmade*.

Now, you understand that even the world's most expert quilters will shy away from a quilt four inches thick, right? They know such a monstrosity cannot fit under the foot of their sewing machine. They wouldn't even attempt to create one. But Donna figured we could tie the two layers together with soft yarn here and there, all the while keeping the down from whooshing out into the room in a snowstorm of tiny feathers.

Cory was happy to take the kids to the zoo to give me a few hours with my sister, so I packed up my sewing kit and took off. When I arrived, Donna looked like an Arctic wild woman, the sort who might just marry the abominable snowman. White fuzz clung to her hair, face, clothing—every surface of her body. And just think: She had invited me to come over and share this questionable fate.

"You know, you can pick these up for thirty bucks or so at a white sale," I started to remind her. After all, she has plenty of discretionary income.

"Nonsense," she said. "I want these girls to learn how to do things themselves."

"Then why aren't *they* over here, making these themselves?"

"Well, I'm showing them by example."

Ah. And where in the handbook does it say each girl has to have a down-filled pillow-topped mattress?

"Besides," Donna continued, "I want them done right."

And there it is—the number-one reason why some people never learn to delegate. They cannot fathom an event where every detail is not up to their exacting standards. Once you delegate, you lose control over all kinds of details. You end up with napkins that don't match, microphone cords that don't reach, and the wrong kind of lettuce in your salad. Of course, you also have people who are acquiring skills, becoming dependable, feeling needed, and learning teamwork. But those goals are waaay behind the goal of a perfect event, so nondelegators continue to do everything themselves, and "perfecting the Saints" moves comfortably to the back burner. It's a lot like parenting. If you can't abide a crookedly made bed and you make all your kids' beds for them, they never learn to do it themselves.

But it's useless to argue with Donna, so I dished up the chicken salad I brought over to sustain us in this task. We finished it off with some coconut cake, then I sat down at her quilting frame and dug into the project. The quilting frame was set up in her impeccably decorated living room, a taupe-and-gold tribute to Tuscany complete with a gleaming antique buffet, heavy brocade window boxes, and draperies held in opulent swags by ten-pound tassles. Oh—and, of course, bits of white feather down settling on surfaces where it was undoubtedly unwelcome.

"Are any of the girls allergic to down?" I asked. I was hoping one or two might be so we could switch to a nonallergic poly-something filler that might be easier to work with.

Donna blanched. "I have no idea!"

"Probably not," I said, wishing now that I hadn't even brought it up. "They'll love these."

Donna sighed and kept shoving fluffy down into the corridors we were creating with knots of yarn. I don't know if you've ever stuffed anything, but it usually takes about five times as much stuffing as you think it will. Donna, however, knew this and had mountains of down in plastic bags, piled up like a year's supply of popped popcorn. Should any one of these burst, we could suffocate within seconds.

Suddenly she looked through her front window and gasped. I followed her gaze and saw a man walking across the street, carrying what looked like a casserole covered with foil.

Donna dashed to the window. "No!" she said. "Oh, my gosh. That Lutheran family is taking food to the Wilsons!"

I raised my eyebrows. How was this a bad thing?

"The Wilsons are the neighbors I've been fellowshipping!" Donna said, more than a trace of panic in her voice. "She had a baby last week so I brought in a meal for them."

"And?"

"So now what am I going to do?"

I swallowed. "Be glad?"

"Of course not! This means I've got to do more. I can't have neighbors doing the same thing I'm doing! She has to think we do the most!"

I closed my eyes and tried to process her logic.

"This really makes me mad," Donna said, pacing.

I stared at her. "Mad as in angry or mad as in scientist?"

She pursed her lips. "This undoes all my efforts!"

"How, exactly, does this undo your efforts?"

"Because!" Donna looked at me like *I* was the one with the problem for not understanding what was plainly before me. "If we all take food in, then how does my doing it stand out? I just look like one of the many neighbors."

"Donna, you *are* one of the many neighbors."

"But I want her to see us as special," she said. "And now the Lutherans have cancelled out my meal!"

I stood up and steered her toward a chair so she could sit down and collect herself.

"Nobody is canceling out your meal," I said. "I'm sure it was appreciated, and it was probably the tastiest one she got." This I could actually say with a good deal of certainty, because Donna prided herself on her excellent cooking. "Just keep being your friendly self."

"But it won't work if everyone else is friendly too!"

I wanted to say, "How old are you—five?" But I didn't. Instead I tried to get her to see this from a gospel perspective. "Did Christ run around and tell people not to copy Him? If someone else was kind or charitable did He think it cancelled out His efforts?"

"Well, no, but that's different," Donna argued.

"How is it different?" I said. "Are you honestly competing to see who can be most Christlike—and are you truly mad if someone else shows kindness too?"

Now she glared at me and went back to working on her quilt. I was hoping my words would sink in and show her how ridiculous she was being, but a few minutes later she said, "I'm taking over a lemon cake tonight."

I sighed. "Whatever." Honestly, the thing to do is figure out where all the Donnas live, move in across the street, and have a series of operations and setbacks. You'll have fully catered meals for the rest of your life.

We got all but two of the mattress toppers finished, and I was starting to see double. Donna agreed that we were working "past our best efforts" and assured me she could finish the remaining two on her own. "I owe you," she said, kissing me on the cheek and waving good-bye. I drove home with Neosporin on my pinpricked fingers and wisps of down dangling from my eyebrows and lashes.

A week later I called to see how the girls liked their surprise, but Jerry told me Donna had come down with pneumonia again and was in the hospital. "Good grief!" I said. "Was it from breathing in all that feather down?" Sacrificing your time and talents is one thing, but sacrificing your health to make a totally over-the-top project was taking it entirely too far.

"Oh, no, no," he said. "It's a viral thing. In fact, she really can't have any visitors. But she should be home in a few days. I'm sure she'll recover fine."

"Okay." I sighed. "Gosh, she seemed fine when I was over. Please give her a hug from our whole family, okay, Jerry?"

"I will."

And then I wondered if maybe I could have caught the same bug and was simply in the incubation period before the symptoms appear. But Jerry assured me I was fine and didn't need any tests. I still found it incredible that Donna had suffered three bouts of pneumonia over the years. She probably pushed herself too hard and had too little resistance.

"Can she have phone calls?"

"Of course. I'm sure she'd love to hear from you."

Naturally we all got on the phone and wished her well, and then the kids made a giant get-well card that we delivered with some flowers to the hospital's reception desk.

Sunday one of the Scout leaders gave a talk in sacrament meeting about their latest high adventure. I watched as Hayden's and Joshua's eyes grew round while they imagined the tales of daring—climbing the sheer face of a giant cliff, braving the scalding rays of the sun, melting snow for drinking water, surviving on a measly granola bar and an orange every day.

"Oh, please," I whispered to Cory, "housebreak a Chihuahua; then I'll be impressed." I must confess I spent the remainder of the talk imagining Scout badges for truly needed life skills: scouring an oven, repairing a lawn mower, diapering two toddlers at the same time, negotiating with a cable company for a lower rate, going on a vacation with three kids in the backseat who cannot abide being touched by the other two, making an entire Thanksgiving feast and then running interference for in-laws who despise each other, attempting to help with homework you didn't understand the first time you encountered it twenty years earlier, or cleaning up after a child who has simultaneous diarrhea and vomiting. Okay, that last one may be gross, but it's real life. Hey—how about a badge for hand-stitching a dozen down-filled pillow tops for mattresses?

I should mention, of course, why I had streaks of deep red paint in my hair during that same meeting (here's another badge those Scouts ought to earn).

The previous day I had decided to repaint our front door—not a new color, just a fresher, brighter version of the crimson it was. I set up, taped off the hardware, laid down a drop cloth, and then painted the whole door a rich crimson. Then, so it could dry without sticking to the doorjamb, I left it propped open about four inches. It was still wet and gleaming when the plot thickened. Good old Freckles spotted a family having an afternoon stroll with a baby in a stroller and two dogs on leashes. He bolted past me, squeezed through the door, and raced out to bark loudly enough to scare them out of their wits. Peanut, of course, was right behind Freckles, yapping her head off like a wind-up toy at full volume.

I chased Freckles down and found that he was now half maroon, his entire left side covered with paint. As I dragged him back to the house I got paint all over me, including in my hair. All the while I was screaming at Peanut and shouting apologies to my neighbors—the very people I had promised the missionaries I'd fellowship. Great.

And then I saw my door. The bottom half was now covered with white fur, looking like some kind of Graceland tribute. I threw Freckles into the house and tried to grab Peanut, but she evaded my grip and raced joyfully around the front yard before Joshua chased her into the house.

Now I had to get rags and wipe off the entire bottom half of the door. But dog hair doesn't come off as easily as paint does, so the furry paint dried as I was working. This meant I now had to sand it. I still couldn't get all the hair off. So I repainted the entire door, and now it had a curious "texture" here and there. It looked worse than before I started.

Once that was finished, I turned around to see my ridiculous dog getting crimson paint all over the beige carpet. That was when I finally realized I should have cleaned up the dog before tackling the door, but I was so intent on wiping the hair off before it dried that I wasn't thinking. And Peanut was still leaping around in circles and yapping with glee.

That's how I came to have crimson paint in my hair for church on Sunday. Short of showing up with a tattoo, this is possibly the only way to catch the eye of our ward's young women: Look like you're trying some daring new hairdo.

But I digress. In the middle of Relief Society the bishop popped his head in and motioned me to come outside. As one of the counselors, I was sitting up front, but I slipped out as discreetly as I could.

Bishop Gentry leaned in and whispered, "Sister Barnes has just passed away."

"No!" I whispered back. Not Sister Barnes! Without question she was the favorite sister in the entire ward. At eighty-three she was everyone's ideal woman—the kindest, sweetest, funniest, brightest, most beloved lady most of us had ever met.

"It was heart failure," he said. "Her daughter was visiting from North Dakota. Evidently only the family knew there were some medical issues."

My eyes filled with tears as I listened.

Bishop Gentry went on. "They'd like to have the funeral this Wednesday, if we could. Apparently they want to choose all the speakers and the music; you'll just need to coordinate with the family for food and such."

And then I realized the Relief Society president was on vacation for another week, so the responsibility would fall to me.

"I'll take care of it," I assured him. When I went back in I slipped the teacher a note saying I'd need five minutes at the end of her lesson, and I hurriedly scrawled out a sign-up sheet for babysitting, salads, bread, ham, desserts—and, of course, funeral potatoes. When the teacher wrapped up her lesson I apologized, then broke the terrible news to our sisters.

The shock wave was palpable. None of us had expected to lose this cherished woman so suddenly. She was literally the one we all looked to for direction in a crisis—if she was strong and confident, we knew we could be too. If she said this is the prophet's counsel on a certain issue, then that's what it was. She was the one we all wanted to be when we grew up. And now she was gone.

Some of the women cried, others comforted, but everyone wanted to help in whatever way was needed, exactly what Ruby Barnes herself would have done. The sign-up sheet came back stained with tears but filled with love.

By Wednesday we were ready—well, physically ready, but never emotionally ready. Even when a wonderful daughter of God goes on a joyful journey home again, it's still agonizing for those left behind. The void she leaves is vast and raw and stays that way for a long time.

And as much as I dislike funerals, it was therapeutic to work with her family on planning one for Sister Barnes. Not surprisingly, all of her children radiated her same enthusiasm for life, even in this crisis. Their love of the Lord was obvious and their gratitude for their mother was inspiring. Again, I felt a twinge of longing that Ted could come back and provide the missing puzzle piece in my own family, the one who could make our family as whole and strong as Sister Barnes's family was.

It reminded me of the talks we hear from time to time about what constitutes real peace. It isn't to be free from anxiety, trials, or adversity. It's to rejoice in the gospel and keep our faith *during* those same setbacks—to have a calmness about us even when life seems to be caving in.

The stake center was filled to overflowing, the chapel and cultural hall both packed as if this were stake conference. Chairs were even set up on the stage and in the hallways.

And then something happened at the funeral that, I think, jolted everyone there. Her eldest son gave the first talk and began by asking a favor. "Would everyone who knew Ruby from her seniors' complex please stand up?" A scattering of thirty or so people rose.

"Would everyone who knew her from the Garden Guild please stand up?"

Another two dozen arose.

"Would everyone who knew her from being a hospital volunteer please stand?" At least thirty people stood.

On and on it went—everyone from her quilting group, everyone from her book club, everyone from the League of Women Voters, everyone from the library where she read to children on Saturdays, everyone from her kickboxing class (!!) and, finally, everyone from church.

Tears were streaming down my face as I got to my feet and realized everyone in that room was standing because they knew her and loved her from some way she had served them. In the midst of epidemic excuses (I'm too old, I'm too tired, I'm too busy, I've already served) here was a woman who "got it." She was doing the Lord's work night and day, never complaining and never leaving it to somebody else. She was taking missionary work to the next level and getting out into the community exactly as Church leaders have urged us to do.

A quote by Bishop Glenn L. Pace from his October 1990 general conference address was shared, and it perfectly summed up Sister Barnes's understanding of service. "In humanitarian work, as in other areas of the gospel, we cannot become the salt of the earth if we stay in one lump in the cultural halls of our beautiful meetinghouses," Bishop Pace had said. "We need not wait for a call or an assignment from a Church leader before we become involved in activities that are best carried out on a community or individual basis."

In life she impressed us, and in death she inspired us— motivating us to rejoice to the end, not just to endure. I will never forget the lesson I learned at, of all places, a funeral. And I vowed to repeat her legacy—or die trying!

That night I was still glowing from the love that radiated through the chapel that day and the example I so wanted to match. As Cory and I got into bed, I told him I wanted to make a concrete plan for Ted.

"I've been fasting and praying for him, and keeping his name on the prayer roll at the temple, but I just feel there must be more we can do," I said. "What would Ruby Barnes do?"

Cory smiled. "I think she'd do what you've been doing. You can't force a bud open."

I sighed. "No, but I just think we need to formulate a plan. A step-by-step plan of action."

"This is not like packing a suitcase," Cory said, lovingly stroking my cheek. "I know you're all charged up and energized by Ruby Barnes, but you can't make Ted fit your schedule."

"Why not? Why can't we plan a whole series of events that would culminate in asking him to come back?"

Cory smiled. "Do you really think he doesn't know that's what you want?"

I sighed. "How can he just let the years roll by like this without doing anything?"

"It has to be his choice."

I raised myself up on one elbow. "I hate—"

"Don't say you hate agency. It's a key component of the plan of salvation. And you fought a war for it. You're still fighting a war for it, in fact."

I slumped back down onto my pillow. "Some things suck."

"You tell the kids they can't say that."

"Yes, but they really have nothing to complain about," I said. "This thing with Ted is a spiritual emergency."

"Oh, I'll agree with that," Cory said. "I once told him he's on thin ice—I mean, God forbid he should die, but none of us knows when our time will come, and you want to live in a state of readiness."

I turned to Cory. "What did he say?"

"Nothing. Just smiled and patted my shoulder."

I rolled my eyes. "That is *so Ted.* He has no sense of urgency."

"But nobody has a sense of urgency like the OverAchiever family," Cory said. "Admit it. You guys are the most impatient people on the planet."

"It's been decades! How long are we supposed to wait?"

I could almost hear Cory smiling in the darkness. "As long as it takes."

"But I need to *do* something," I said. "I can't just twiddle my thumbs while I wait for a bolt of lightning to hit him. Although I will admit I have prayed for that."

"And for him to find and read his patriarchal blessing, which he did. And for him to meet up with high school friends who were good examples, which he did."

"And nothing has shaken him up and gotten him on track!" I whispered. For years I prayed that some wonderful priesthood holder would take him under his wing and make Ted his personal project. Didn't happen. Then I prayed for years that some glorious LDS girl would take a liking to Ted, forget what she'd heard all her life about marrying a returned missionary, and bring him back into the Church. In fact, I was still praying for that.

"You've got to relax and let things happen in their own time," Cory said.

"Relax?" I sat up, astounded. *"Relax?"*

Cory shook his head. "I knew that would be the wrong word to use."

Now I was building up steam. "I haven't been able to relax in twenty-five years! How can anyone relax when a family member is lost? Are you not aware that we are living in a state of emergency?"

"Oh, geez, *you* should have been the lawyer. Lie down, Syd, and try to . . . I don't know . . . exercise faith or something."

"I do have faith. I just feel we should do all we can—"

"And you have." Now Cory sat up and put both hands on my shoulders. "You need to calm down."

"I am the only person having the proper reaction to an emergency," I said. "Everyone else needs to calm *up*."

"There's nothing we can do that we aren't already doing," he said. "And I wish to heck Ruby Barnes hadn't died, so I could call her up and have her tell you so."

"But we can't," I said, "because she goes to bed at eight-thirty." And then I realized how truly and completely Ruby was gone, and I burst into tears. Cory got out of bed, came around to my side, and held me against his chest.

"I know," he whispered into my hair. "I know."

"I miss Ruby." I sobbed. "And I'm going to miss Ted in the hereafter."

"No you won't. He'll come around," Cory said. "He will. Just hang on a little longer."

"I'm going over and slapping the daylights out of him," I said.

Cory laughed and smoothed my hair. "I might join you. He's costing me sleep."

Now I took a huge breath and released it. "I'm sorry. I know you have a ton of work tomorrow. Sometimes I just—"

"I know. It's hard."

I got up, blew my nose, drank a glass of water, and got back into bed. Long-suffering should actually be spelled *loooooong*-suffering.

As Cory finally drifted off to sleep, I stayed awake, blinking and watching the clock on my nightstand flip from 11:21 to 11:22. I remembered Ted saying, "One, one, two, two, Boogie Woogie Avenue" when I was a little girl. What was that from? A cartoon? A crazy movie? And then I remembered. It was a song by the Spinners.

And that's when I decided to put a spin on this whole thing and pray a different sort of prayer for Ted. I prayed he would be held up at gunpoint, his life would flash before his eyes, and he would be shaken into coming back to church.

Chapter 5

Within a week Donna was back home, healthy as ever. She reported that her young women were completely bowled over by their mattress toppers and couldn't believe she had given them such a lavish gift. Every one of them had written her a glowing thank-you note, and Donna had already installed them in a scrapbook.

"You do know that you've set the bar impossibly high for your successor," I said.

"And for my neighbors," she crowed, not aware that I was pointing out a possible problem with her scheme. "I gave the Wilsons a soup-of-the-week card."

"Wait a minute," I said. "You're making fifty-two weeks of soup—"

"Oh, no, just for six weeks," she said.

"Well, that ought to show those pesky Lutherans," I said.

"That's ri-ight," she sang, completely missing my sarcasm.

I sighed. There was no reining in this woman. Heaven help the poor family who moves in with no apparent needs or problems. It will drive Donna berserk.

Three weeks later we had the missionaries over for dinner and, as it turned out, entertainment. The first bit of entertainment was provided by Peanut—who, every few evenings, rediscovers that we live in an echo chamber. Let me explain.

Sacramento has a plethora—that's right, I used the word *plethora*—of rivers and wetlands. We bought a house that backs up to one such "nature preserve." Within a very short time we found that *nature preserve* is merely a field-trip term for a swamp with thickets of cattails and just enough standing water to create a petri dish for malaria. We should invest in the mosquito repellant industry.

Every time I leave the house, half a dozen endangered species swoop at me. Granted, these are all birds given marvelous descriptions by the Audubon Society, but they do not care about that. All they want is to star in a remake of Alfred Hitchcock's *The Birds*. That, and poop on my car.

They have built nests all around the eaves and are churning out babies like Keebler cookies. But these babies are not anywhere near as quiet as cookies. They cheep as if the nest's on fire and are convinced that all humans, coming and going, are wingless enemy invaders who must be stopped by any means necessary—or, at the very least, by pecking out their eyes.

As it turns out, beavers have also discovered the wetlands and are building dams. They cannonball into the pooled water with a resounding thump so loud you think a car must have swerved off an overpass and landed in your backyard.

Coyotes are making a feast of all the neighborhood cats, rabbits are chewing up all attempts at gardening, and field mice are having a field day—which is, in fact, where they got the name. Okay, I made that one up, but they are having a field day.

On top of this, the wetlands have created the ideal setting in which Peanut can have an imaginary friend. Here's how it works. Peanut barks in the direction of the wetlands. The banks slope upward, so within about a second her bark comes echoing back to her. But does she realize it's an echo? Of course not. She has the IQ of a coconut, so she thinks it's another dog barking back at her. And so Peanut barks again. And darned if that other dog doesn't bark right back. If Peanut gets more ferocious sounding, so does this smart aleck across the creek. This racket escalates *ad infinitum* and eventually involves neighbor dogs until you pull Peanut into the house by her collar and slam the door. Of course, that also echoes.

So no sooner had Peanut regaled the elders with her mental illness than the phone rang and it was Ted. Once again, I need to give you some background.

Ted's job description, as you may recall, is "maker of all manner of lamps from junk found in assorted—and sordid—locations, including the city dump." But to scavenge at a landfill, you can't just wander in and start poking around. They won't allow it. You need to take a load of trash there and pay to get in, as if on legitimate business.

So from time to time, Ted places an ad in the paper for "hauling." He then carts off the debris from not-so-big demolition sites, landscaping projects, and renovation jobs. He's husky and fast, two qualities that make folks glad they hired him to clean up their driveways and side yards.

Mom is mortified that he's driving loads of trash around at his age when he could have made so much more of his life, but she has backed off considerably in the last few years, and almost visibly bites her tongue when Ted comes over.

I picked up the phone, saw it was Ted, and put it on speaker mode. "I hope I'm not calling at dinnertime," Ted said.

"It's okay," I said. "We have the missionaries over, but we're just finishing."

"You serving Chicken Problema?"

I scowled. "It's Chicken Poblano, Ted." This is my standby dinner for the missionaries and Ted loves to mangle the name. "So what's up?"

"Well, guess what happened at the dump today?"

I spend approximately zero seconds thinking of such possibilities, so of course I had no idea.

"I got held up at gunpoint," he said.

Immediately I recognized this as the answer to my prayer, so I whirled around, a huge grin on my face, and stopped just short of giving Cory a high five.

Everyone stared at me like the lunatic I was actually impersonating, not sure if they should be more shocked that Ted was held up or more shocked that I seemed so pleased about it. Cory, in particular, looked at me like I needed my head examined, jumped up from the table, and dashed over closer to the phone.

"Ted, it's Cory. We're all on speakerphone. Are you okay?"

"Oh, yeah, I'm fine," Ted said.

Cory looked at me as if to say, *See? This* is the appropriate *question you should have asked.*

Ted went on. "They arrested the guy."

"So tell us what happened," I said. I just knew the story would end with Ted saying, "And it shook me up so much I've decided to come back to church this Sunday."

The kids had all jumped up from their chairs and were huddled around the phone, shushing each other so they could hear.

"Well, I had just brought in a load of broken asphalt," Ted said, "and just as I was shoveling the last of it out of the truck, suddenly I felt this jab in my side, and I turned and saw this transient guy. Pretty scruffy looking. Smelled like whiskey. He was right up against my ear and said, 'Gimme your wallet.'"

The kids all gasped.

"Then what?" Ellie and Hayden cried in unison, their eyes like a little row of hubcaps.

"So then I turned," Ted said, "and I looked down and saw his pistol still shoved up against my ribs, and I told him to hold on, because my wallet was in my truck."

Even the missionaries were riveted, listening with open mouths.

"And I was thinking I'd better remember what he was wearing in case I could give the police a description, but it was just some ratty jeans, a gray T-shirt, and a black jacket, which was also what *I* was wearing."

"Good grief," I said. "Then what?"

"So the guy kept his gun against my side as we kind of inched our way to the driver's-side door," Ted said, "and I told him my wallet was in the glove box. So while I leaned across the seat to open the glove box, I was at the perfect level to kick him in the groin. So I did, and he doubled over."

"Whoa," Cory said. "He could have shot you, Ted."

"Yeah, but he was drunk and wasn't expecting me to kick him," Ted said.

We were all shaking our heads in amazement.

"Did he fall to the ground?" Ellie asked.

"After I banged the door against his head," Ted said. "Then I grabbed the gun and kept one foot on his neck to keep him down. The work boots helped. So then I laid on the horn and whistled for help and a coupla guys who work there ran over, and they called the cops."

We were all talking at once, mostly saying "Wow" and "Whoa."

"But the bummer is that I had to go with the police to the station to file charges and sign a bunch of forms," Ted said. "So I didn't get to look for any materials."

Materials = Trash = Art Supplies.

"You were nearly killed and all you're worried about was not getting any stuff at the dump?" I gasped.

"Well, it was a wasted trip," Ted said.

I was waiting for the part where white-robed angels suddenly appeared, pointed at Ted, and sang (or said—I'm not picky), "Time for you to get back into the gospel, Ted."

Maybe his awakening came at the police station. "So, you had to have a moment when you realized this was a huge deal," I said.

"Oh, sure," Ted said. "Probably the minute he stuck his gun in my side. And it was all kind of surreal. I mean, I've never thought out what I'd do in a situation like that, but suddenly I was like a trained spy or something." He laughed, amazed that it worked as well as it did.

"Was your wallet really in the glove box?" Cory asked.

"No, it was in my pocket," he said. "But I wanted some way to get the guy over by the door so I could hit him with it."

"I can't believe you made up the glove box story so fast," Ellie said.

"That was pretty quick thinking," Cory agreed.

"Well, I guess your brain clicks into gear in an emergency," Ted said.

"It's so odd that some guy would hold you up at a landfill," Cory went on. "How had he planned to get away?"

"Well, good question," Ted said. "I mean, it's not like it's a quick zip out of there—it's kind of a long, winding road to the entry gate, and then a good distance to the freeway. I figure he probably lives there at the dump, hiding out from the landfill workers, and maybe he found a gun."

"Well, drunks don't always think things through." Cory smiled.

"Thank goodness," I said. "You're so lucky you're alive, Ted."

"Yep. Anyway, just thought you guys could use some excitement."

"Wait—" I said. I was still hoping for the life-changing moment in all this. "So did you feel like you had a guardian angel or something? I mean, you were really being watched over, huh?"

Ted paused, seeing through me completely (again). "Syd, if I have a guardian angel, he has a punctuality problem, because it seems to me he should have kept me from getting held up in the first place." The kids and the missionaries all laughed.

I sighed. "Well, we're very grateful you made it through such a dangerous ordeal," I said.

"And now I've gotta get another hauling job so I can get back to the dump," Ted said.

Right. "I don't suppose the police would have let you go shopping for a few minutes before coming with them to the precinct," I said.

"Nope."

Alas. We hung up and went back to the dinner table, where two fresh-faced elders were still wide-eyed over the story. I could just imagine their letters home: "Dear Family, We had dinner with one of the weirdest families yet. First their dog was barking at its own echo, then their brother called and told about being held up at gunpoint while scavenging at the city dump. And the wife served us Chicken Problemo."

I pictured frantic mothers writing back, "You stay away from that family! They have a dangerous lifestyle." Years from now some descendant will be reading his dad's missionary journal and will learn all about our crazy family. Just like that, we will live on in infamy.

That night as we were getting ready for bed, I explained to Cory that I had prayed for Ted to get held up. I confessed that's why I had been so excited at his phone call.

"Good grief, Syd."

"Well," I continued in my own defense, "you can't just pray away someone else's agency, but you can pray for circumstances that could lead to right decisions." I splashed my face.

Cory shook his head. "And you thought being held up at gunpoint would make Ted take stock of his life and become active again?"

"That's right." I dried my face on a towel.

"You are a twisted woman. Has that ever happened in the entire history of the world?"

"I'm sure it has," I said, popping out my contact lenses. "Are you kidding? People fall off ladders and lose their jobs and have all kinds of experiences, and it makes them reconsider how they're living. Like a guy with a heart attack who says it was a wake-up call."

"Yes, a wake-up call to eat right and exercise."

"And come back to church," I said. "Sometimes it takes a serious accident or something."

Cory held me, smiling and still shaking his head. "Well, at least your prayers are being answered."

I lit up. "I know! Isn't it great?" I threw my robe over a chair and knelt down next to the bed for prayers.

Cory sighed. "I think the message is for you, though—not for Ted."

"What's the message for me?"

"To stop interfering and let Ted come around on his own."

"Oh no, that can't be right," I said. "If we let Ted do this on his own it might never happen."

Cory clasped my hands and said a prayer, then climbed into bed. I stayed put for a moment while I added my own private prayer. And this time, I turned up the heat. This time I prayed for Ted to get into a terrible, though not fatal, accident.

Chapter 6

WELL, YOU'RE NOT GOING TO believe what happened at church the next Sunday. Okay, maybe you'll believe it. First of all, we sat down and opened our sacrament meeting programs, and across from the meeting's agenda were the ward announcements, starting with SAVIOR OF THE WORLD AUDITIONS in a bold font at the top of the page.

"What on earth—" I whispered to Cory. "I do believe that position has been filled."

Cory glanced over at the program and smiled. "I think it's a stake musical," he said.

"Well, it might have been worded a little more clearly," I said. "Some quotation marks, at least. What if there are investigators here? What will they think we're teaching?"

Cory slipped the program into the hymnal lest I find further cause for alarm and put his arm around my back. After the meeting, the older kids all shot out in various directions to their classes while Cory and I put one of Juliet's shoes back on. I was just tucking a quiet book back into the diaper bag when the unbelievable thing I referred to happened. Sister Moretti, the Primary president, came up, beaming. But it wasn't one of those *Boy, am I happy to see you* beamings; it was an *I have bad news but if I smile when I tell you, it might soften the blow* beaming.

"Syd," she said, leaning over the bench in front of us, "I just thought I'd better tell you before someone else does."

Oh, great—it's anybody's guess what *this* could be.

Sister Moretti leaned in to whisper. "Last week in sharing time we were talking about being honest, and Joshua mentioned that you, well, sometimes stretch the truth."

"What?"

"Actually, both of your boys said it."

Now Cory was leaning in as well. "What? What did they say?"

"Well, Joshua said his mom—" here she stammered, then finally just went for it—"lies all the time, and Sister Hammond said, 'Oh, I'm sure your mother doesn't lie, Joshua,' and then Hayden spoke up and said, 'No, she really does.'"

Cory and I had matching dropped jaws.

"I'm sure it's nothing, but I just thought you should know," Sister Moretti said. Then she actually *winked* and walked away.

Cory and I spun to face each other. What on earth were our boys talking about? And in front of the entire Primary?

"I'm getting to bottom of this," Cory said, and we both headed straight for the Primary room.

"Good grief," I whispered as we walked. "This is like the time Ellie told the whole Primary that I drive like Cruella de Vil."

Cory smiled. "Except that happens to be true."

We called our little comedians out into the hallway and gave them Sister Moretti's report.

"But, Mom," Joshua said, the same way he pleads to stay up another half hour, "you do!"

"Yeah, you do," Hayden said, one of the few times he has ever been in complete agreement with his brother.

"Oh, really?" I snapped. "And just how do I do this?"

"With your split sticks," Joshua said.

Now Cory and I just stared at the two of them. "Her what?" Cory asked.

"Those numbers she makes up," Hayden said. "Like 85 percent of all boys who have good manners get more money from the tooth fairy."

"And only 10 percent of people in car crashes live if they're not wearing a seat belt," Joshua added.

"Her *statistics*," Cory said. Then he looked at me accusingly.

"And the one about half of all fatal diseases coming from dirty socks that didn't get put in the hamper," Hayden said.

Cory stared at me. "You didn't."

My face was flushing now, but my pride had grabbed the steering wheel. "Every one of those had a noble motive," I said. "Name me one statistic that didn't lead to better behavior."

"All made up." Cory looked like he was cross-examining me in a courtroom.

"Well," I said in my defense, "I'm pretty sure the one about eating your vegetables is true."

Cory looked at Hayden, who said, "She says 85 percent of kids who eat their vegetables grow taller."

"I can't believe you've been saying these things," Cory whispered.

"Oh, like it's a crime," I said, trying to tap dance my way out of it.

"It's one of the commandments," Hayden said, sticking one little finger in the air for emphasis.

"It's not the same thing as lying," I hissed.

"It is absolutely lying," Cory said. He turned to the boys. "I'm sure Mom will not be doing this again." He squeezed my hand.

"Fine," I said.

"You're saying that through clenched teeth."

I took a breath and opened my mouth. "Fine," I sneered. Then I leaned down to the boys. "How did you guys know I was making up those statistics?"

And now Hayden gave me an absolute Cory look, as if I surely didn't think I was fooling him all this time. "We know your tricks, Mom."

And now my mouth shot open with surprise. How could they possibly have known? I was totally convincing!

"We will not be talking about Mom during Primary," Cory said as he marched them back to singing time. As the door swung shut he turned around and shook his head at me. "I can't believe you resorted to manufactured statistics. That's got to be one of the worst parenting blunders—"

"Hey, Mr. 'Bet You Can't Get Dressed Faster Than I Can,'" I scoffed.

We headed for our Sunday School class. "Challenging a child to a race is not the same thing as lying," Cory whispered.

"It's tricking him into doing what you want him to," I said.

Cory just shook his head, though I could see he was trying to stifle a smile. "My wife, pleading guilty to fraud."

"Oh, please," I whispered as we opened the door to go inside. "Ninety-eight percent of all mothers do it."

That afternoon Ted came over for dinner, since he promised a friend he'd help with some car repairs on Monday night. Of course, the boys had a heyday telling him all about their mom "getting into trouble" for lying. Ellie was torn between taking my side and joining the obviously more fun side of hooting and hollering over Mom's lapse in judgment.

Ted kept eying me, smiling and shaking his head between bites of my ginger-glazed salmon.

"Oh, no you don't," I said, pointing at him with a serving spoon. "People who have no kids do not get to criticize those who do."

Ted slathered butter on his dinner roll. "I haven't said a word."

"No, but you were thinking it."

Now he smiled. "People who are not psychic do not get to read the minds of those who are."

"You are not one bit funny," I said. "Or psychic."

Fortunately, this was a new word for the kids and got them off the subject of my, shall we say, misrepresentations.

Then the kids began telling their Uncle Ted that my funeral potatoes heralded in another death this week.

"They did not *cause* a death," I clarified.

Cory then told Ted about Ruby Barnes's amazing funeral and all the people standing up who had known her through her community involvement.

"I think at mine they'll say, 'Would everyone here who bought a lamp they regret buying from Ted OllerVanKeefer please stand.' The whole place will be on its feet."

We all laughed. I glanced at the French horn lamp in our family room, which Ted made from the horn Cory played in high school. I still loved it.

"She was lucky to go fast," Ted said. "I mean, that's how we all want to go, not lingering and suffering."

We all agreed, and Ted said, "I've got that whole Alzheimer's thing figured out."

"You do?"

First we explained Alzheimer's to the kids then Ted explained his foolproof plan. "When I get really old I'm going to hire some hit men. I will instruct them to come and visit me every six months and ask me who they are. And when I can't remember, they're to shoot me."

Cory and I laughed until we were crying. "Syd knows what she wants on her headstone," Cory said.

I sipped some water. "It's going to say, 'I told you we should have stayed with the group.'"

"Good plan," Ted nodded.

I went on. "I'm also leaving behind a list of approved anecdotes the children can share at my memorial and a list of forbidden anecdotes that will disqualify the teller from any inheritance."

"Such as the fake statistics," Cory said.

"That's right." I looked at the kids, who were grinning. "And I want a party instead of a funeral. But you can display a photo of me at my prime."

"Which photo?" Ellie asked, clearly the future family matriarch who will oversee such plans.

"Well," I said, "I'm actually still hoping for a prime, so it hasn't been taken yet."

"I was talking to a lady in my trailer park awhile back," Ted said. "You know my friend Eva? Well, she went to a friend's funeral where the main thing the kids talked about was the wonderful chopped liver sandwiches their mom always made. Until then, Eva had worked for years to get her fudge recipe just right, and was probably the best fudge maker in the whole city, but she stopped that very day. She said no way was she going to have a fudge-themed funeral. So now she tells her kids that if they want fudge, they can buy it."

"I kind of wish I'd known this before the friend's funeral," I said. "I could have ordered some killer fudge from her."

"Me too," Cory agreed.

"Wow," Ellie said, "I'll bet Aunt Donna's will be a scrapbook-themed funeral."

I shuddered to think what my theme might be—shamelessly lying and making up statistics?

"Mom's will be about funeral potatoes," Joshua said, and I actually sighed with relief.

Cory laughed. "Your mom has a lot more accomplishments than that."

"But there have been an awful lot of funerals lately," I said.

"And too much talking about death," Ellie said.

"Hey, it's part of life," Cory said. "And we're lucky we know it's just another doorway, and that we'll all be together in the hereafter."

I forced my eyes not to look at Ted's and instead surveyed the smiles on our kids' faces. Had Ted smiled that way as a youngster when our parents taught him about eternal families? Would our kids wander off the path like Ted had, even though they knew the truth? My eyes watered and I began clearing dishes.

Fortunately Ellie jumped up and pulled Ted by the hand over to the piano so she could play him her latest song. Cory lifted Juliet from her high chair and began wiping it down. The boys began vying for attention from Ted by banging on the lower keys and crawling through his legs, but Ted managed to grab both their heads and steer them to his sides so they could listen to Ellie's song. It reminded me of a sniglet I'd read in grade school called *Noggin Navigation* in which parents steered kids by turning their heads. I so wished Ted could be a father; he would make a wonderful one.

The very next week he called and said, "I'm bringing the kids a surprise." Ted's voice was cutting out on my cell phone, so I stood up from where I'd been digging weeds and tried to find a clearer spot.

"What is it?" I asked.

"See you in an hour or so."

I finished filling the last trash bag then peeled off my gloves and washed up. Juliet had been playing beside me, bobbing up and down in a baby bouncer, and the boys were fighting over who got to bring her inside. Joshua prevailed, and soon we were all watching at the front window for Ellie to come home from a neighbor girl's birthday party and for Ted to drive up.

"What do you think it is?" Ellie asked, immediately over the news that the birthday girl's arm was in a cast from falling out of a tree the day before.

"I'll bet it's a rifle!" Hayden said, his mind whirling with the possibilities. As if I'd let Ted hand a firearm over to a seven-year-old. Or an any-year-old.

"Maybe it's a black stallion," Joshua said, having recently seen the movie and become fixated on the adventure of a race through the Middle East.

"I hope it's a time machine," Ellie gushed. "Do you think there really could be time machines, Mom?"

"Stephen Hawking does," I said. "I was reading an article last week where he said it might be possible to warp time and space enough to allow a traveler to return before he leaves."

Ellie's eyes danced. She thinks anything Stephen Hawking says is right up there with the gospel. Unless, of course, he questions God.

"As soon as they figure it out, I'm going," she said.

"Good," I told her. "You can tell Uncle Ted—" and then I caught myself. "You can tell him hello when he's still a little boy."

"That would be so cool," she said. "I could say, *Hi, I'm going to be your niece one day!*"

I smiled and suddenly realized that all the people we think are crazy might just be time travelers.

Ellie is wildly in love with numbers. From the time she learned of their existence, she ascended (descended? side-scended?) into a happy little world of ratios and logarithms, even sharing an elaborate equation with me—including lovely arcs—to prove the uselessness of cleaning her room.

I, on the other hand, recoil mentally whenever a digit appears. I think it started with story problems in elementary school. Well-meaning teachers would hand out preposterous questions—and I assumed the goal was to see who could go the longest without screaming.

"You have one apple and you want to share it equally with seven friends," such questions would begin. And that's when I would stop and imagine such a ludicrous situation. Who planned so poorly as to have only one apple when seven friends arrive? My solution was ultimately to make a small Waldorf salad, though I wasn't convinced this would be anywhere near enough food for eight people.

"You found one grape and want to share it with nine friends," one question said. Immediately I would try to picture this. Who are these people? Street urchins from the Dickens era, covered with soot, who find in the gutter one grape that even the dogs won't eat and who decide to share it with nine friends? I decided they ought to spend less time socializing and more time working so they could buy everyone a grape. I wrote, "I would not do this" for my answer. What was next—dividing a pea into twenty pieces with a scalpel? Were we going to be given microscopes for the next batch of story problems?

And then along came fractions, criss-crossing operations, long division, and ultimately *algebra*—which, if you haven't pictured a bra made of algae yet, means you haven't given enough thought to that word. Worst of all, they were now mixing letters with numbers, a sacrilege if ever there was one.

My best friend in junior high was a girl named Audrey, and she shared my distaste for things mathematical. But in her case, it was because she was an artist. When given a long equation with a little numeral two elevated above the other numbers to indicate "to the second power," all she could think of was how stranded that awkward two looked, like a lone painting hung too high on a giant wall. When she finally solved the equation, all that was left was the little two floating like a lost balloon.

Numbers people have other amazing abilities as well. They're like savants of a sort for whom musical training is a snap. I have yet to meet a math whiz who is not also a gifted pianist. And juggling! Who would have thought juggling went along with this? But it does. I know of an AP calculus teacher who tells his students that whoever masters juggling will get an A in the class, and he's invariably right. Evidently the same gymnastics your brain goes through in order to juggle are the same processes it needs to understand calculus.

All I can think about are the bruised oranges that will result as folks try this at home—dropping the fruit time and again until it cannot be shared with even one friend, let alone forty-nine.

Ted's white pickup truck pulled into the driveway, and we all saw three huge cardboard boxes in the back. The kids went running out.

Ted told them to meet him in the backyard, and one by one he brought the boxes around the house.

"The boxes are really noisy!" Joshua gleefully reported, as if this were a good thing.

"Uh-oh," I said. We all dashed out the back door.

And then Ted opened the boxes. Out flapped three humongous, honking geese, larger than could fit into any oven known to man.

You think you have seen large geese, but you also thought you knew the ultimate scrapbook queen, didn't you? Each of these geese was the size of a Saint Bernard.

And, speaking of dogs, naturally Peanut and Freckles had heard the commotion and were now charging out their doggie door to join the fray. And then the sprinklers turned on.

I ducked back into the house, plopped Juliet into her playpen where she could watch us out the window, and dashed back outside again.

Now we had three overjoyed but hyped-up children, one possibly insane uncle, two euphoric dogs convinced they were champion geese hunters, and a husband just coming home from work. All but the husband were thoroughly drenched by the sprinklers.

Cory walked onto the back patio and said, "What on earth—"

A helicopter flew overhead at exactly that moment, and I was sure it was filled with folks enforcing the zoning codes that forbade farm animals in this area. I just knew that at any minute they would blast through a bullhorn, "You with the geese—put your hands up."

The kids, Ellie leading the way, decided to name them Uncle Waldo, Amelia, and Abigail, after the *Aristocats* movie—the geese, not the police.

Then the kids decided to hug them. The geese initially ran away but quickly reconsidered and decided to ATTACK.

Ted then explained—as if he were suddenly the host of a nature program—that you have to take a swing at the geese with something to keep them from getting aggressive and turning on you. This is why he was able to get these oversized geese for free on Craigslist. Marvelous.

Ted and Cory began waving rakes and brooms at the geese. Cory was shouting for Hayden to bring his golf clubs out of the garage. And Ellie had gone inside for food, since these animals were obviously starving.

"Can't you get them to fly away?" I shouted over the mayhem.

"They can't," Ted called back. "Their wings are clipped."

What kind of deranged lunatic clips the wings of a group of ATTACK GEESE, thus rendering them unable to fly away from you?

Ellie was back now with the food: torn-up tortillas, Corn Pops cereal, wheat bread, and cornmeal, all served on paper plates—a lovely touch that I'm sure was appreciated by our heathen guests.

No takers. Wait. I take that back—the dogs were gobbling up the tortillas and Corn Pops as fast as they could while avoiding being speared by a goose beak.

The squawking . . . honking—whatever you call it was now escalating and I knew my phone would be ringing with irritable neighbors any second now.

"We've got to get them out of here," I shouted to Ted. Already our porch was filling with goose poop, and it was starting to look like we'd been strafed by a low-flying plane that dispensed white shoe polish.

Peanut was throwing up unchewed Corn Pops and Juliet was crying inside the house.

"I thought we could release them into the wetlands," Ted shouted.

Yes! Yes! Saved by that bug-infested quagmire at last. The kids thought it was a perfect idea, where the geese could swim happily about and have babies in the spring. They opened the back gate and began waving paper plates and brooms at the geese to shoo them in the right direction. Cory managed to get the dogs back inside, I got Juliet to stop crying, and finally the rest of the gang came in for towels. And then the sprinklers turned off.

"Well, that was excellent timing," I muttered.

Cory was wiping off his dress shoes now, loosening his tie, and giving me the evil eye.

"Hey, don't look at me," I said, setting the table for dinner. "Ted called and said he was bringing the kids a surprise."

Cory headed toward the laundry room to give Ted a piece of his mind, but I caught him by the arm. "No," I said. "You can't!"

"Or what—he might not come back to church? Please. He'll either come back for the right reasons or he won't." Then he looked into my eyes and exhaled loudly. "Fine. I won't say anything."

Just then Ted came around the corner, carrying his wet tennis shoes and socks. "I know, I know," he said. "No more surprises."

"Thank you," I said. "And for what it's worth, I'm glad it wasn't a rifle, a black stallion, or a time machine."

"Huh?" asked Cory and Ted in unison.

"That's what the kids were hoping for," I said. "I, of course, was hoping for three gigantic, violent geese, and got exactly what I wanted."

"Your sarcasm is registered," Ted said.

I bent my head back to stretch my neck, which I was just now realizing was kinked with tension. The kids came in, still ebullient over their temporary new pets, and Ellie decided to make up a song about them on the piano.

Cory handed me an envelope he had just picked up from the mailbox. It was from the Department of Motor Vehicles. "Looks like it's time for you to renew your license," he said.

I tore it open and, for the first time in years, it said I had to come down in person rather than renew my license through the mail. "But," I said, "I only have to do an eye test and provide a fingerprint, so that's not so bad."

I ushered everyone to the table, we asked a blessing, and I dished up some stew I'd had simmering in the slow-cooker. Cory passed around some crusty rolls and a butter dish.

"I liked your goose composition on the piano," I said to Ellie. She beamed.

"Here you go, Tootsie Pop," Cory said as he spooned a soft bit of potato into Juliet's mouth. "Maybe one day you'll play the piano like your sister and brothers."

"But maybe not," Ted said.

I frowned. Why wouldn't she play the piano? The whole family played the piano.

"I don't like it," Hayden said.

"What?" I was shocked. "I thought you liked Mrs. Denmore." She was the piano teacher we had come over on Wednesdays to teach one kid after another, and I thought everyone more or less enjoyed it.

"I can't think when I have the music in front of me," Hayden said.

Then, out of the blue, Ted high-fived him. "Welcome to the club," he said.

"What club?" I asked. And Cory, who played almost every instrument in existence, was equally perplexed.

"Didn't you know about this?" Ted asked. "Didn't you ever wonder why I was the only one who didn't play piano?"

To be honest, since I was nine years younger than Ted, he was almost twenty by the time I was old enough to wonder.

"My teacher was Mrs. Dibble," he said. "I'll always remember how exasperated she got but how she tried to hide it. Finally she talked to Mom and Dad and told them not every kid can learn to play the piano."

"What?" I said. "I thought it was like reading—you just learn it."

Ted shook his head. "It's a decoding thing. It's in the hard wiring of the brain. You look at the notes, but you can't make your fingers find the coordinates. It's almost easier to close your eyes and just play by ear."

"I do that!" Hayden shouted, clearly thrilled to discover he was not alone.

"Decoding?" Cory asked.

"It doesn't mean he isn't smart," Ted said, ruffling Hayden's hair. "It's just that not everyone can see a written note and then find it easily on a keyboard. And processing chords is even harder. So you put kids like me on a one-note instrument, like a saxophone, and we do fine."

Now that I thought about it, I could remember Ted dabbling with a saxophone when I was a little girl.

"Mom, please?" Hayden said. "Put me on a saxophone instead."

"There are lots of options," Ted said. "Just a thought."

I looked at Cory and shrugged. Who knew this? It certainly might explain why Hayden struggled with math.

"Fine with me," Cory said.

Ted turned to me. "There are all kinds of physical reasons for what we don't like," he said. "Like you, Syd. You don't like ball sports."

I raised my eyebrows. This was true. Running was one thing, but throwing and catching always frustrated me.

"It's because you're nearsighted."

"What?"

"You and I were the ones who got the bad eyes," he said. "And a year or so ago I was at the eye doctor's and he asked if I liked sports. I told him I'll watch a game on TV now and then, but I'm more of a fisherman/hiker type. He handed me a card with simple drawings on it—a dog, a ball, a tree, and so on. Then he gave me these dark sunglasses with tiny holes all over them and said, 'Put these on and then look at the card.' He asked me if any of the pictures appeared to be floating in the air. I told him all of them did."

We were all eager to hear what this meant.

"So I took off the glasses and he said, 'You have terrible hand-to-eye coordination. You were probably never very good at ball sports."

"And that's true!" I exclaimed. "I mean, for me too."

"He said if a professional baseball pitcher put the glasses on and looked at the card, all the images would appear to be flat on the card. Those guys have awesome hand-to-eye coordination."

So it's like they're cheating, I wanted to say.

"So all this time I thought I was just a klutz, but it was my eyes!" I felt a mixture of relief and aggravation at all the time I had wasted trying to excel in sports that I never could have mastered. "They ought to test kids in the schools," I said. "And not make them waste their time with ball sports, but get them doing something they really can do."

"Yep," Ted said. "We would save a lot of self-esteem for a lot of kids."

"Well, I'm going on the bandwagon," I said.

"What a surprise," Cory deadpanned.

"Seriously! Teachers should know about this! I can't tell you how many times my PE teacher compared me to Chad and Neal, like I was some kind of grand disappointment on the volleyball court. I'm calling the school board tomorrow."

Cory nodded. Having lived with my gusto for ten years now, he was not at all fazed by my announcement.

"They already have machines that analyze what sports your body is best built for," Ted said. "So it's not like this should be all that surprising to the PE teachers."

"Exactly!" I said.

"And," Cory added, "since you have nothing else to do now that your statistics manufacturing firm has dried up. . . ."

I smiled, refusing to take the bait. "Precisely. This will fill that gap quite nicely, I think."

Chapter 7

WELL, AS YOU MIGHT IMAGINE, lobbying a school board to test children for athletic aptitude was not a pursuit that found immediate success. But I did bend a few ears and get a letter to the editor published in the local paper. Finally I printed up flyers and sent them to several PTAs. If I could get parents passionate about this, then they could take the message to their own PE instructors.

While I was stuffing the last batch into envelopes, Ted called.

"Hey," he said. "Don't you need to go to the DMV before your birthday?"

"Yes, why?"

"Wouldn't it be a lot easier without the kids?"

"Sure would," I said, thinking Ted was volunteering to watch them for me.

"Well," he said, "how about I meet you at Mom and Dad's, you can drop off the kids, and then we can go to the DMV and grab lunch someplace?"

"Yes! I would love that," I said.

His timing was perfect; the kids were due for a visit with my parents anyway, and the DMV wasn't far from their house. This would also give me some great time alone with Ted.

Mom and Dad lived in a wonderful old Dutch farmhouse built in the city. We loved the stone exterior, the windowpanes and the white shutters, the high ceilings and the deep kitchen sinks. Many times we had wondered about the original builder—had he come from Europe? Or was he a city boy who found a bride from the prairie and promised her a farm-style home where they could raise hardworking children?

Whatever the history, we loved growing up there and now loved seeing the grandchildren race over its hardwood floors and play hide-and-seek in its generous closets. Mom kept the place immaculate, yet it was never stuffy. The kids knew they could romp and play, and as long as they reentered through the "mudroom" after being outdoors, it stayed clean as a whistle.

Mom and Dad were in their midseventies now, and while Dad had long ago retired from his job as a banker, they kept as busy as ever. Their latest plan was to serve a mission, and they were actually just filling out their application.

Mom had both brownies and cookies ready and waiting when Ted and I arrived, and the kids couldn't wait to dig in. As they raced to the kitchen I handed off the diaper bag to Dad, and Juliet to Mom.

"She's teething," I said, "but should be okay. I have a couple of frozen teething rings in the bag if you need them."

"Don't you worry about a thing," Mom said. Then she looked at me and frowned. "That's how you're having your picture taken?"

My hair was up in a messy bun after a morning of housework, and I wasn't wearing any makeup except for some lip gloss. I had thrown on an old T-shirt and some jeans, but since it was only a vision test and thumb print, I wasn't worried. I explained that to Mom, then Ted and I took off.

"You know why I'm accompanying you," Ted said as we walked through the door.

"Because you love my company?" I teased.

"Because I know how you hate the long wait at the DMV, and I'm keeping you from killing somebody."

I smirked. "Why does everyone think I'm this—" I groped for words, but kept coming back to the same ones—"impatient, out-of-control, crazy woman?"

"You mean everyone who knows you?"

I rolled my eyes. "I expect no more of others than I do of myself."

Ted laughed. "I still remember your report cards from grade school. 'Sydney has a hard time being patient with her peers.'"

"Well they weren't even trying!" I blustered. "I still remember that."

Ted shook his head. "You need to learn to relax."

There was that hideous word again! I could feel my blood boiling. Besides, what kind of word is *relax,* anyway? How can you RE-lax if you haven't laxed in the first place? And who wants to be lax? Isn't sloth one of the seven deadly sins? And isn't *relax* just a synonym for "be slothful"?

Wisely, I had made an appointment. This saved the local news from having to cover a mass homicide. CRAZED MOTHER OF FOUR TAKES OUT 42 CITIZENS AT LOCAL DMV.

"I have a sterling driving record, you know," I told Ted. "They usually mail me my new license."

Ted smiled. "Mine's stainless steel."

At long last I was called to window fifteen for my vision test. I wear contacts and passed with flying colors. And then, in a horrible twist of fate, the gruff woman behind the counter told me I had to be photographed!

"No, no," I explained. "The letter just said vision and finger-printing."

"It also said a photograph," she argued. And even though she had not read the same letter I had received, I do recall a bit of fine print at the bottom, so I decided not to wage a war over this.

"Oh, my gosh, Ted, look at me!" I pulled the bobby pins out of my bun and now my hair stuck out at odd angles. I tried to smooth it down, but there was nothing I could do about my face—with no makeup we pale OllerVanKeefers look like big rounds of Jack cheese. And without mascara my eyes look scarcely open. So there I was, looking like a squinty mole with generous cheeks, wearing a fright wig.

The woman snapped my picture and I stepped away for the next impatient person to have his turn at a mug shot. As I was walking away, Ted said, "You have a piece of chocolate on your lips."

What? I reached up to pull it off, and it wasn't chocolate at all, but a BIG BLACK GNAT that had flown into my lip gloss, choked on it, and died. I realized that my new photo was going to look like a squinty mole who had just gorged on a wad of cheese, with hair looking like I've got my toes in a light socket and am being electrocuted, and with a BUG stuck to my lips!

Ted laughed his head nearly all the way off and I stormed out of there, vowing *never* to get pulled over anytime for any reason.

"I am shredding that thing the second it arrives," I said, still furious as we pulled into a mom-and-pop burger joint. "I'll have to call and reschedule another picture or something."

"I think they just send you a duplicate. And it costs thirty bucks or something," Ted said.

I fumed. "Then I'll get an ID card separate from a driver's license, and that's what I'll show if I have to."

"They might still use the same photo," Ted said.

"You don't even know!" I hissed. "You're just guessing the worst possible thing you can think of!"

He shrugged and glanced at the menu. "So what are you having?"

"Same old."

"Me too."

We got our usual burgers with grilled onions and mushrooms. We sat down with our curly fries and I tried to forget the hideous hour I had just endured.

"So Ellie is quite the math whiz," Ted said. "She was telling me about time travel."

"I think she traveled back to the premortal existence and stood in all the math and music talent lines," I said.

"Wonder what she'll be."

I dipped a fry into some ketchup. "If boss of the world is open, I think she'll apply for that."

Ted laughed. "She'll probably be a physicist. Or a concert pianist." He took a sip of his chocolate shake. "Did I ever tell you what my aptitude test said I'd be good at?"

"No—what did it say?" I remembered my own saying I should become a lawyer or a horse rancher.

"Mom threw a fit," Ted said, smiling as he remembered it. "The top choice was—are you ready for this? A clown."

"A *clown*?"

"Yep." Now Ted laughed. "Oh, you should have seen her. She ran into the bedroom with Dad and slammed the door and I could hear her through the door saying, 'No child of mine—'"

I laughed. I could absolutely imagine her saying that.

"So then," Ted said, "she marched down to the school and shook the test at them and said *clown* shouldn't even be one of the choices. She had a whole list of horrible jobs that shouldn't be on the list: Bank robber, hit man, loan shark, graffiti artist, drug dealer. Of course the school officials told her that they never recommend those things. And then she said, 'Exactly. And neither should you recommend CLOWN.'"

I was laughing so hard I couldn't even drink my root beer. "Like being a clown is a crime!"

"I know! But the thought of her child growing up to be a clown was enough to send her over the edge."

I was still laughing as I had another fry. "I kinda wish you had done it," I said.

"Nah," he scoffed. "I wasn't interested in that. But I did dress up as one from time to time, just to get her goat."

"You're a terrible tease," I said.

"Yep. But 'tease' wasn't on the job list. If it had been, that's the job they would have recommended for me."

"No doubt." I could picture my poor mother nearly having a stroke as Ted showed up in floppy shoes and a rubber nose.

Ted swallowed the last of his burger. "She really needs to lighten up," he said.

"Do you really think she's going to change at seventy-three?"

"No, but I don't have to go along with her agenda," he said.

"Her agenda?"

"You know, have perfect little Mormon kids who grow up and have more perfect little Mormon kids."

"Am I being insulted?"

"No—you know I love your kids. I'm just saying she has this formula for how everyone needs to live, and not everybody fits her mold."

"Ted," I said, "I'm hoping my kids turn out well and stay strong in the Church, and that their kids do the same—it doesn't mean I have some 'agenda,' as you put it. It's living the gospel plan and hoping your kids all do the same."

Ted shrugged. "But with her it's a compulsion. There's no room for anyone who doesn't get straight As or doesn't earn his Eagle or—"

"Wait a minute," I said. "Ted, you were probably the smartest of all of us. You easily could have earned your Eagle, probably ten times over. You didn't go with the program because you didn't want to be told what to do."

"Who does?"

"Most people don't do the opposite just because their parents guide them in a certain direction."

Ted sipped the last of his shake, gurgling sounds coming from the bottom of his glass. "But it wasn't *guiding*. That's the problem. It was *forcing*."

"How come it didn't bother any of the rest of us?"

Ted shook his head. "I know you think I have an authority problem."

"Well," I asked, "do you?"

He smiled. "I may. I just don't like something being shoved down my throat."

I sighed and patted his arm. "I never felt I was choking on it. I'm really grateful that Mom and Dad set standards, made us go to church—I'm *glad* they were strong, Ted. Can't you see it as something they shared because they truly love it and believe it?"

Ted folded and refolded his napkin. "I don't like being controlled."

I smiled. "You don't see how, by rebelling, you're still giving them all the power in your life."

Ted looked at me, puzzled.

"You're only in control when you're making decisions freely, for yourself," I said. "If your choices are a *re*action, instead of an action, then Mom and Dad still control you."

I could tell this was a new idea to him.

"Anytime your choice is to do something *against* what you've been told," I went on, "then you're not really acting independently. Am I making sense?"

He nodded but was still frowning.

"Anyone who rebels is still letting the other person control him," I said. "For me, it's simple. Either Joseph Smith was telling the truth or he wasn't. And whether someone else tells me *to* believe it, or *not* to believe it, I pray about it and decide for myself. What others tell me to do is immaterial."

I waited a minute to let him mull that over. "Basically," I went on, "if you know Christ suffered to buy our freedom, to make it so we could come home again   and be together forever as a family— then I say thank Him every day for that incredible gift, and live to be worthy of it."

Now he was chewing his cheek.

"Forget about getting even with Mom and Dad for whatever they did that hurt you. You couldn't please them? So what? Please the Lord." I could feel a lump in my throat but pushed past it. "It's not the end of the world if you happen to choose the same thing they did. It doesn't mean they won a battle of some kind."

Ted cleared his throat and stood up. "Okay, missie," he said. "We should go now."

I sighed. I knew I was on the brink of preaching, but I really felt Ted needed a different perspective and needed to realize how childish it was still to be rebelling against his parents.

Mom wasn't the only one who needed to lighten up.

Chapter 8

OF COURSE, THE WHOLE FAMILY went into a frenzy of jubilation when I told them I had a gnat stuck to my lips for my driver's license photo. The kids kept pointing out other winged creatures that could find their way onto my lips. Then Cory e-mailed me as "Bugsy" from work, Donna emailed an online poster of Jodie Foster with a butterfly on her lips from the movie *The Silence of the Lambs,* and I got a text from Ted saying he was impressed by my gnatty attire. I know one thing for sure: That license will never see the light of day when it finally arrives in the mail.

Oh—and on the way home I told Ellie, who was riding shotgun, to listen to the new hands-free cell phone gizmo clipped to my visor. Not all states have cell phone laws, but California does, so I had to find a way to comply. I didn't want a bluetooth because 1) I thought it might get tangled in my hair, and 2) they look like giant, shiny, hissing cockroaches (though after my new photo, insect wear may become all the rage).

This visor gadget, which looks like a garage door opener, is *way* more distracting than a cell phone, but far be it from me to break the law—and even farther be it from me to risk getting pulled over and having to show that hideous new photo. The gizmo has several buttons you have to press to turn it on and to hear a caller, but I keep the law and use it. When the call is finished, you have to push two more buttons—one to end the call and one to shut off the device.

The problem is, it doesn't shut off. Instead, you hear a woman speaking Hawaiian. I kid you not. Have you been to Hawaii? Have you noticed that every other road reminds you of Donald Duck's nephews, Huey, Luey, and Dewey? Of course they're spelled Hui, Lui, and Dui. And you've seen the King Kamehameha Highway, right? But let's be honest: Not that many people actually speak Hawaiian, so I'm puzzled as to why a cell phone company would produce a product that has a Hawaiian feature. How large a market can that be, after all?

Every time I hang up, this woman says, *"Seha Kameha."* I cannot get her to stop. I press additional buttons, but all I get is *"Seha Kameha."*

So I called Ted to thank him again, and when I hung up, I said to Ellie, "Listen to this. It's a Hawaiian lady on my speaker thing."

"Seha Kameha," the woman said, right on cue.

"See that?" I shouted. "She's speaking Hawaiian. *Seha Kameha.*"

Ellie sighed. "She's telling you to say a command."

OH, FOR CRYING OUT LOUD! All this time I had control of the universe and I didn't know it? And what kind of command does she want? Get Ted back to church? Lower the price of gasoline? Make this car a Ferrari? Give me back my teenage body? To think I'd had a genie clipped to my visor all this time!

And now I wonder about the whole Hawaiian language—have I just been listening wrong all this time? Maybe King Kamehameha never even existed, and folks were just trying to say, "Come here! Come here!" Even that Merry Christmas phrase, *Mele Kalikimaka,* probably just refers to a leak that needs mopping. We simply need youthful translators, that's all.

"I can't believe you thought that was Hawaiian," Ellie said. The boys were howling with laughter in the backseat.

"I can't wait to tell Dad," Hayden was saying, as if tattling on one's mother is perfectly all right (I thought we settled that after the Primary fiasco).

Joshua was looking through a book my mom had given him about zoo animals. "Is this one of the leopards Jesus healed?" he asked, turning the book to the front for Ellie (or me, the driver trying not to be distracted) to see.

"That's a lion, Joshua," Ellie said. "And Jesus healed *lepers*, not *leopards*."

"Oh. I thought he healed the spots off."

"That book is wrong," Ellie said.

"Do you mean it's wrong that the spots were healed, or wrong that a lion is a zoo animal?" I asked.

"Objection," Ellie said. "Compound question."

This is what you get with a lawyer for a father.

"I don't think the book says anything about Jesus healing the lion," I said.

"It's just pictures," Joshua added.

Ellie took a deep breath, as if facing a jury. "What's wrong is that lions are animals in Africa. That book makes it sound like a zoo is where a lion normally lives."

"True," I said. "A zoo is not a native habitat."

"Then why is Joshua reading this book?" Hayden asked. "It's just going to confuse him."

Ellie snatched the book away. "I agree."

"Hey, gimme that back!" Joshua was now leaning forward and kicking Ellie's seat.

"Give your brother the book," I said. "And tell him the story of the lepers."

I thought this would end the quarreling, but, in fact, now Hayden and Ellie were arguing about the particulars of the story and who got to tell which part.

"Oh, for crying out loud," I said. "Do you think Jesus wants people fighting over the details of that story?"

"Here come the statistics," Ellie said.

"I am not giving you any more statistics," I said. "But I can guarantee a lot of people don't know the point of that story."

"What's the point?" Joshua asked.

"That only one of them thanked Him," Ellie jumped in ahead of Hayden.

"I was going to say that!" Hayden said.

"So we can agree, then," I said. Sheesh! You think a cell phone is distracting while you drive? Try having three kids bickering about a Bible story.

"It's about gratitude," I said. "Church leaders have told us it's one of the most important virtues. And in the scriptures it says the sin of ingratitude is one of the most serious of all sins."

"Well *I'm* grateful," Ellie said, apparently for the benefit of any unseen visitors taking notes.

"I know you are," I said. "All you children are very good at saying thank you and counting your blessings."

"Especially on Thanksgiving," Hayden said.

Yes, especially then. Like most families, we always go around the table on Thanksgiving and allow each person to share something he or she is thankful for. You think right away of the gospel, your family, good health, our free country—so this should be a slam dunk, right?

Not with our family. We started alternating between Cory's family and mine when we first married, and whenever it's his family's turn, they gather at our house. Naturally, Ellie produces the event with pine-cone turkey placecards, pilgrim hats, and a cornucopia. And, unfortunately, ever since she learned the alphabet, she has insisted we list our blessings alphabetically.

And that's where the whole game breaks down and becomes, dare I say, the stupidest tradition imaginable. You are no longer searching your heart for a sincere expression of thanks, but groping wildly for any noun that could possibly start with *J* or *X*. Within seconds, nobody even thinks of "family" for *F,* but "flu shots," "fries," and "flame throwers."

All the kids become raucous wise guys, talking with their mouths full of mashed potatoes and praying the letter *U* will land on them so they can say "urinals" (which Cory actually chose one year and defended by saying they're handy to have).

Not only this, but everyone suddenly becomes a grammar expert and argues over whether hot rods can count for *H*, since *hot* really modifies *rods*—and, using the same logic, whether garlic bread can count for *G*. Garlic bread, incidentally, is suddenly extolled as a wonderful food and the kids take a spontaneous vote that we should add it to the menu next year, as if my exhaustion is up for expansion. That year a discussion of other foods I should be willing to get up at 2 AM to prepare included fried rice, ice cream, carrot cake, cotton candy, and fried chicken. These were agreed on as if we had hired circus clowns to revise the food pyramid.

Cory's family loves to join in, and that's probably why I don't put a stop to the shenanigans every year. I guess I realize that while this might not be the touching, spiritual moment I grew up with, it is nonetheless a bonding moment of laughter and good memories, and that counts for a blessing right there.

When we got home the phone message light was blinking. Ellie had run into the house ahead of me as I was unbuckling Juliet's car seat, so she had already listened to the message.

"Sister Monahan wants to take you and Dad to dinner!" Ellie reported. "Are you going?"

I sat Juliet down. "Why wouldn't I?"

"Mom, are you kidding? She's crazy! And so is Brother Monahan."

"Fine with me," I said. "I like crazy people."

Ellie whistled. "Good luck!"

I listened to the message. Sister Monahan's voice was both gravelly and loud, booming into the kitchen, so I turned down the volume.

"Hi, Syd," it said, "Frankie and I want to thank you for taking us to our doctor appointments, so we want to treat to you some frozen yogurt. Can you and Cory come tomorrow night? Can you pick us up?"

I chuckled, called her back, and told her we'd be happy to pick them up and go to the local yogurt shop. Now I just had to brace Cory.

The Monahans were baptized several years ago by eager elders who didn't stop to make sure they were accountable—and since both of them are, shall we say, a few cans short of a year's supply, who knows? I'd been driving Bertha Monahan to her psychiatrist appointments and both of them to Frankie's parole officer appointments for years. They're on state aid, do not own a car, and have no means of travel unless someone picks them up. And everywhere they go they speak about prison and "loony bins" loudly and freely, garnering stares in supermarkets, government offices, hospitals, and everywhere else you can name. On top of that, they both shout over each other and there's no way to get a word in.

In my own twisted mind, I think it's funny. Bertha has all her belongings in plastic bags, stapled to the wall. Frankie occasionally answers the door in one of Bertha's housecoats, and they can both walk to the bowling alley, where they've been asked not to come back "even though we were just cheering them on," Bertha bellowed. It's like a comic strip come to life.

It's not as if they haven't made progress. Frankie no longer looks through people's windows, Bertha has stopped shoplifting (I think), and they both have AA sponsors who've been keeping them off booze. Their attendance at church is sporadic, but always with hilarious excuses—

Frankie: I put hair dye on my leg hair and didn't realize how long it needed to set.

Bertha: I used my pantyhose to clean out the bathtub after Frankie got in there covered with motor oil.

Frankie: I knocked a hole in the ceiling with a golf club and the lady above us is threatening to sue us.

Bertha: I think two of the women at church have their eye on Frankie and I don't like it. (The chances of this, without making up any statistics, are approximately zero—maybe even less than zero.)

Frankie: I accidentally took Bertha's medicine and can't walk straight.

I know these stories have to be legit, because who could make up such crazy scenarios? And I'm glad they found each other and managed to stay together against all odds. And I'm glad I asked to be Bertha's visiting teacher, because I don't know if anyone else would find this as entertaining as I do.

"I am not going for yogurt with those two," Cory said as he took off his tie up in our bedroom after work that evening.

"You have to," I said. "They're trying to thank us for driving them around."

"Well, let them thank you," he said. "You're the one who's done the driving."

"Oh, please," I said. "Let them have some moment of normalcy."

"She's calling *us* for normal?" He rolled his eyes.

"Everyone at their senior complex hates them."

"I wonder why."

"But imagine having no friends," I said. "We've got to do this."

Cory sighed and I knew he was caving in. "The things you get me into," he muttered.

And thus it was that we drove over to the Monahans' and picked up Frankie and Bertha for frozen yogurt on two-fer night. The minute we walked in we drew stares. Frankie was wearing some sort of rubberized top with overalls, and Bertha had put on a hot pink floppy hat for the occasion. Both of them were wearing bedroom slippers.

"Order whatever you like," Frankie yelled (for some reason mentally ill people shout all the time, but I haven't figured out why).

Then we all sat down with our bowls of yogurt and toppings. Frankie and Bertha proceeded to argue with each other about one of Bertha's split personalities and whether it had truly disappeared.

Bertha told me her doctor had written "borderline psychosis" on her chart once, but I hadn't mentioned the split personality thing to Cory because I saw no benefit in telling him that Bertha's other "self" was a lady of the evening, shall we say.

Immediately I could feel panic rising in my chest.

"Yeah, that was Geraldine, all right," Frankie was saying.

"Was not," Bertha shot back.

Do not ask, "Who's Geraldine?" I mentally tried to transmit into Cory's brain.

"Well, you think she's gone, but she's not," Frankie said.

I tried to catch Cory's eye, but he was riveted on their discussion. *Do not ask, "Who's Geraldine?"* I shouted inside my head. And then, to Frankie, *Change the subject!*

"Let me tell you," Bertha said, "you do not want Geraldine to show up."

"That's for sure," Frankie bellowed.

No! No! Do not ask—

And then it happened. Cory swallowed a bite of yogurt and asked, "Who's Geraldine?"

I pictured an airliner hitting the side of a mountain.

And then Bertha muttered, "Never mind. You can't afford her."

"She's Bertha's other personality," Frankie said. And then he explained to Cory the sort of living Geraldine made.

Cory's jaw nearly hit the table. He looked over at me, and now all I could do was stare into my lap. *Hey,* I thought to myself, *I tried to stop you from asking, but no—you had to go there.*

Frankie's eyeglasses fell into his yogurt *twice,* and he put them back on, yogurt dripping down his cheeks.

Cory, sitting across from Frankie, was becoming more and more distressed with every passing minute—and I must admit, I was finding this most hilarious of all. What is it about the discomfort of our husbands that we wives find irresistibly entertaining?

Frankie's teeth fell into his yogurt next. Horrified, Cory visibly jumped an inch.

"Your teeth fell out," Bertha yelled.

"Oh, they're not going anywhere," Frankie said and continued eating around them.

Cory stared in disbelief. I noticed other customers craning to get a look at these two and a couple of the employees whispering in the corner.

"So then," Frankie shouted as if he had been in the middle of a story, "I got pulled over. This was back when we had a car. And wouldn't you know it was the *same cop* as before!"

Cory was trying to catch my eye to motion that we should leave now, but I wouldn't let him do it.

"Not the very same cop," I said, just egging Frankie on.

"Yep, the same one!"

Bertha was leaning back and licking the inside of her bowl to get the last drops of yogurt. Cory's eyes darted from one of them to the other, as if he were watching a ping-pong match.

"Tell about your AA sponsor," Bertha shouted.

Cory was in agony, but Frankie proceeded to tell about how his sponsor came to the jail and tried to convince the officers Frankie hadn't been drinking, "but tranquilizers count the same," he said.

Aha. "Did you know, Cory," I asked, "that you can get a DUI for drugs as well as for alcohol?"

Now Cory refused to look at me and just tapped his empty cup with his plastic spoon.

"Did you want some more?" Frankie bellowed.

"No, no, I'm full," Cory said. "In fact, we should probably be going—"

"What?" Bertha said. "We just got here! You haven't heard about the time we were sleeping under the freeway and got attacked by some crazy guy."

So they proceeded to tell that story, and halfway through Bertha stood up to adjust her underwear and tell about a strange rash she gets if her underwear is too tight. I could see Cory willing himself not to picture this.

At last the rest of the yogurt customers had gone and Frankie and Bertha were out of stories. For now.

We dropped them off and waved through the car windows as they headed to their apartment.

Cory slumped over the steering wheel. "You are a SAINT!" he shrieked. "How can you stand this? You drive them all over town?"

I couldn't help laughing at his agony. "I think they're funny," I said.

"Funny as a cracked radiator. Those people are insane! How can you do this?"

I kept grinning as we drove along. "I liked the teeth falling out."

Cory shuddered. "That was revolting."

Now I laughed all the harder. "You hated it."

"And that amuses you."

I smiled. "For some odd reason, yes."

"Maybe all three of you are crazy," Cory said.

I nodded. "That would explain a lot." And I certainly have the driver's license to prove it.

Chapter 9

I CAN UNDERSTAND CRAZY PEOPLE SOMEHOW. It's kind of like talking to children—you go where they are. You take an interest in their concerns and passions and share their world for a while, trying to see things from their perspective.

But while I tolerate Frankie's and Bertha's high-volume conversations, I have no patience with other people who talk loudly for no reason. Allow me onto my soapbox for a moment.

I was in a department store with the kids a few days later waiting to pay for a gift for Cory's mom, whose birthday was coming up.

Suddenly the woman ahead of us recognized someone in line far behind us. Instead of asking me to hold her spot and walking down to her friend, she chose to yell, "Hey, Sandy! I didn't know you were coming here! How are you guys?" My face was nearly blown off by her volume. My ears are still ringing.

Simply put, people are louder today than when I was a young girl. They shout in your face (though not necessarily *at* you), they chat loudly on their cell phones in restaurants, they even barge into conversations and start one of their own. No one seems to take note of the proximity of others' ears; they just tighten the ol' diaphragm and belt out their thoughts.

As the mother of four kids I know a thing or two about loud voices. But this isn't a genetically louder phenomenon I'm witnessing. It's the absence of all concern, and even awareness, that we could be assaulting someone else's hearing, to say nothing of annoying them beyond all levels of polite society.

Even at church while the prelude music is playing before sacrament meeting, I've noticed leaders frequently asking us to keep our voices down and be reverent—that didn't happen years ago. People knew to whisper in the chapel.

I see two main culprits. One is that parents don't seem to be teaching manners and etiquette like they used to. Kids used to be taught that there were "indoor voices" and "outdoor voices." Screaming and hollering were fine on the playground or the beach, but once inside, civilized people brought it down a notch.

Instead, kids today are raising their voices above the blare of the TV or video game, and parents are calling back, "What? I can't hear you," which encourages the child to shout even louder. Gone is the concept of physically walking up to the person you wish to address and keeping your voice down.

Gone also is the notion that women should have soft, mellow voices. Whiny, shrill, and nasal qualities used to be trained out of a girl by the time she was old enough to date. It was called *elocution.* Today these hideous, high-pitched sounds are ubiquitous. Perhaps it was sexist to tell a woman not to be piercing or boisterous, but are we better off for it? Do we think, *Good; you be yourself* when we hear someone who sounds like a cat with its tail caught in a door? I'm just saying.

I think the second culprit is preschool. Two whole generations of children have now been scooped up and deposited in a group setting during their formative years, forcing them to howl like wolves anytime they want attention—which, if you've raised children, you know is relatively often. Preschool noise levels rival the stock exchange at closing, and if a child wants to be heard, he has no choice but to shout above the mayhem. He then takes these skills into elementary school, where they serve him well in the classroom, another crowded setting. Soon he's yelling above the soccer game crowds, the racket of a bunch of kids skateboarding, and the iPod rap song that's pounding his hearing right out of his head.

Malls have filled with noisy youth, some of whom will even shout into a store, "Hey—what time is it?" to anyone who will shout back. Yowling youngsters are not removed from restaurants by thoughtful parents anymore. Instead, Mom and Dad assume these sounds are welcome ambience in any dining establishment— after all, it takes a village, right? And people are shouting to friends on buses and airplanes as if the other passengers simply don't exist.

Ellie saw my dismay as the woman kept shouting to her friend, and she finally covered her ears with her hands.

The woman saw this and interrupted her shout-fest to say to me, "What a rude girl!"

"Excuse me," I shot back. "You're yelling and she's protecting her hearing. We should all be covering our ears."

Now the woman, ready for a fight, said, "No wonder she has no manners! Look at her mother!"

"*You're* the one with no manners," I said. "You should have walked back there to talk at a normal level."

"I think an apology is in order," the woman growled.

"Fine," I said. "I accept."

I think this is the closest I have ever come to being assaulted. I was saved only because it was this woman's turn at the cashier. A timid woman behind me tapped me on the shoulder and whispered, "Good for you."

"Thank you," I said. Correcting the behavior of the world, one offender at a time—just one more service I offer.

Of course, the kids couldn't wait to tell the (highly embellished) story to their father over dinner.

"And it never occurred to you to turn the other cheek?"

"Are you kidding?" I gasped. "Do cops turn the other cheek when people break traffic laws?"

Cory sighed. "But they're breaking actual laws."

"Rules of etiquette should be law," I said. "Laws, rules—it's all semantics."

"I'd love to see you in a courtroom."

"Well, hang in there and you may get your chance."

Cory laughed. "No doubt."

"Seriously," I said, "someone should hand out rudeness tickets, and that lady should have been arrested. Disturbing the peace, for one."

Cory wiped Juliet's mouth. "And that someone should be you."

"If no one else will volunteer," I said as solemnly as I could, "then I humbly accept this noble duty."

"And it doesn't occur to you that telling someone they're rude is itself rude."

I shrugged. "Sometimes you have to choose the lesser of two evils. And letting someone get away with damaging other people's hearing is much worse than correcting them."

"I like talking with you," Cory said as he buttered a roll. "It keeps me on my toes in case I ever encounter a completely insane defendant."

I chose to take this as a compliment. "You're welcome," I said. "Yet one *more* service I offer."

"Lasagna's my favorite," Joshua said, happily digging into his dinner.

We all laughed because at least twice a week, depending on what we're having, he will announce that chicken is his favorite, or meatloaf is his favorite, or salmon is his favorite.

"I think Mom did the right thing," Ellie said, returning to the earlier incident.

"Thank you, Ellie," I said. "There'll be a little something extra in your allowance this week."

Cory was flabbergasted. "Syd!"

"I'm kidding," I said. "But Ellie's right. I don't have to let complete strangers insult my children. It's a mother bear thing."

Cory nodded. "I agree with you there. Nobody gets to insult our kids. I'm simply asking you to take it easy the next time. Some people are just crazy enough to pull out a gun or something."

"They should pull out an etiquette book and study it." I smiled at Cory, who shook his head.

The phone rang, but we let the machine pick it up—our dinnertime policy. Even so, we could all hear the message.

"Hi, everybody." It was Ted's voice. "Just thought I'd let you know I got a job. I'm going to be the used-car salesman I was always meant to be. Call me."

We all exchanged excited grins.

"This is awesome!" Hayden said, pumping his fist. He was no doubt imagining the shiny, cool cars he could explore.

"Good for Uncle Ted," I said.

Cory agreed. "He'll be great at that."

That Saturday we all piled into the car and went to see him in his new workplace, a huge car lot filled not with used cars, but brand-new, high-priced luxury cars. He had cut his hair, trimmed his beard, and was wearing a shirt and tie.

"You look like a bishop!" Joshua shouted.

Ted gave me a look. "Did you tell him to say that?"

"I certainly did not," I said. "However, you do look a little bishopy."

Ted laughed. "You know, the owner here is LDS."

"Really?" I asked, delighted. Maybe this was finally an answer to my prayers, and a wonderful LDS man would take Ted under his wing. As Ted worked with him every day, maybe his high standards, love of family, and devotion to God would inspire Ted to reach for the same goals.

"Remember, kids," Cory said, "no touching the cars. Somebody had to polish every one of those."

"Aw, let 'em," Ted said. "Other kids get to." He walked us through the lot and the offices where deals were signed. I wanted to meet his LDS boss, but he was out test-driving a car with a potential buyer. Soon we decided to clear out. When a guy is working on commission, time literally is money.

We went for ice cream down the street, and Hayden was bursting with excitement. "Did you see that silver Lexus?" he said.

Evidently every make and model was burned into his brain. And the "new car" smell was now Joshua's favorite smell.

Ellie was most excited about Uncle Ted being all dressed up. And the fact that his entire last name fit on his name tag.

A few weeks later, over some beef stroganoff at one of our Monday night dinners, Ted explained a thorny company policy. They evidently had customers fill out a satisfaction form, and if you didn't get enough "truly outstanding" marks, you were fired.

"Are you kidding?" Cory said. "How many times has anybody bought a car and considered the experience 'truly outstanding'?"

I agreed. Does anyone have even five experiences in his lifetime he would consider *truly outstanding*? What would qualify? The births of your kids, your marriage, your baptism, temple ordinances? What else? What would a salesman have to do to leave you with that kind of a buzz after you've just shelled out a huge hunk of your earnings—throw you a parade? Send you on a cruise? Offer to put your kids through college? Now that would be truly outstanding.

After that explanation, Ted told us he'd been fired for not having enough "truly outstanding" marks.

Our faces fell and the kids groaned. "Oh, Ted, I'm so sorry," I said, giving him a hug. We all felt terrible for him, angry at the dealership, and heartsick that this was another failure Ted didn't need.

I was furious that the LDS owner wouldn't give Ted another chance, especially since Ted was inactive and needed a good example. Now what would Ted think? I just knew this would be another gigantic setback for any hopes of getting him back to church.

He shrugged. "It's fine," he said. "I'll get something else."

We tried to drum up enthusiasm for that idea but couldn't shake off our disappointment. Hayden had especially looked forward to spending lots of time looking at the new cars, and he was visibly saddened.

Ted ruffled his hair. "Sorry about that, champ."

"It's okay," Hayden mumbled. We cleared the dishes, and as Ted was leaving, Hayden went up and gave him an extra-long hug. Then he looked up at his uncle and said, "I still think you're truly outstanding."

Tears filled my eyes and we all agreed with Hayden.

Chapter 10

A MONTH LATER AN OLD high school buddy of Ted's came into town. Ted brought him over for dinner.

"This is Olson," he said, introducing his pal to the kids.

Sean Olson was now forty-three, a bit heavier through the middle, and a bit thinner on top, but still had the mischievous gleam in his eye and the toothy smile that won over all the girls twenty-five years ago. He was married now with two kids in college. He was working as a school administrator in Oregon and had come to town for his father's funeral.

"Oh—you should have called my mom to make her funeral potatoes," Ellie said over dinner. "Hers are the best."

"Wish I had," Olson beamed. His father had lost a long battle with lung cancer, and by the end everyone felt his passing was a blessing.

"Never smoke," Olson said, pointing at the kids.

"We won't, we won't," they promised.

"Oh, that's right—you're Mormons, huh?" Olson said. "I remember that. Then you'll all probably live a long, long time."

"More bread?" I offered him the covered basket and he took another piece.

Olson smacked Ted on the arm. "So what's with you, guy? Why aren't you still doing the Mormon thing?"

Ted laughed and shook his head. "I dunno."

"Hey," Olson went on, "the Mormon kids in my schools are some of the best. You gotta get your mojo back."

My heart was smiling, but I tried not to look over-the-top thrilled to hear this.

"Well, you probably corrupted me," Ted teased.

Olson laughed. "No doubt." Then he turned to the children. "Hey, do you kids know the gorilla story?"

Ted and Olson, along with three other buddies, were enrolled in the same French class in high school (and I pity the poor woman who had to teach them). This gang of five had the brilliant idea to make a movie for their final class project. They wrote up a script, rented gorilla suits, then went around town waving swords and yelling about a gorilla takeover of the universe. But they did it all in French, so no one worried very much.

They asked my dad to drop them off downtown, saying they'd call when they needed a ride home. They called, all right—but not quite soon enough.

Dad picked up the phone and Ted was now asking if he could pick them all up at the capitol building.

"Why, sure," Dad said.

"Good," Ted replied, "because there are a couple of state troopers who'd like to meet you."

My mother threw a fit of worry, of course, wondering what terrible predicament Ted had gotten into. Dad simply drove there as quickly as he could.

It turned out these teenagers had the bright idea to film in the rotunda of the capitol building itself but didn't think to ask permission—something real filmmakers do. So the boys were yelling, waving swords, and stomping around when the elevators opened and two uniformed troopers stepped out with their pistols drawn.

"Put down your swords and take off the monkey suits," one of them shouted. This was all captured on film, of course. Slowly the boys placed their weapons on the marble floor and removed their gorilla heads. One of them was told to turn off the camera and obediently did so.

Thankfully the boys were clean-cut and respectful. Thankfully they did not mention that gorillas are apes, not monkeys. Thankfully one of the troopers had attended their same high school. So they did not get arrested.

Dad's speedy arrival to shake hands also helped, as the boys sheepishly (ape-ishly?) slunk back out of the capitol building with firm instructions to apply for a permit the next time.

In the years since then, of course, security has been amped up, fences have been installed, and no sword-carrying kid can just waltz into the rotunda in a gorilla suit. I like to think that's because of the terrorist attacks, not because of my brother.

But the story didn't end there. The best part was imagining the guy watching the security monitors. Can't you just see him blinking and rubbing his eyes and then trying not to sound drunk as he calls in a report that five gorillas are waving swords and speaking French in the capitol rotunda? Somewhere there is a file containing a report of this evening. And somewhere there is film footage of state troopers doing their job and your tax dollars at work.

Well, the kids giggled with delight at this story. One more swashbuckling escapade of their uncle's to tell and retell every Thanksgiving.

"I'll bet this gets told at your funeral," Ellie said brightly.

"That's a cheerful thought," Ted said. "I can only hope."

"Did Aunt Donna make you a scrapbook of it?" Joshua asked. To our children, every event must be duly reported to Aunt Donna for official documentation.

Ted smiled. "Nope, not yet. I'll have to get her to do that one day."

And then Donna's scrapbooking "hobby," shall we call it, was explained to Olson.

"Hey, my wife did that when our kids were a little younger," he said. "Can you believe she had a separate charge account for the craft store?"

I could believe it. But I feigned surprise at hearing this.

We finished the pork roast and moved on to the German chocolate cake.

"Man," Olson said, "do you people eat like this all the time?"

"Always on Mondays," Cory said and smiled at Ted.

"Ted is my excuse to cook," I winked. "Otherwise it's pasta salad and sandwiches, I'm afraid."

"So how's the job search going?" Olson asked Ted. I liked this guy; he was able to say everything I wanted to, yet with no suspicion of my having put him up to it.

Ted shrugged. "Not a whole lot out there."

"You should be a pirate," Joshua offered. "They get to wave swords too." Obviously that was his favorite element of the gorilla story.

"Pirate of the high seas," Ellie added.

"Well, why didn't you say the *high seas* part?" Ted asked. "Now you've got me interested."

This, of course, got the kids brainstorming for endless possible career choices. So much better than an aptitude test.

"Drive-through comic," Cory suggested.

"How about stepchild to the stars?" Olson said. "You could claim to be the illegitimate child of some rich movie star!"

"Mother would like that," Ted nodded.

"You did a good impersonation of the pope a few Halloweens back," I said. "There's always that."

Ted smiled.

"How about being a taste tester for a donut shop or an ice cream company?" Ellie said. Now that's one we'd all enjoy.

"Be a trapper," Joshua shouted. He'd recently seen an illustration of a man in a coonskin cap with a rifle slung over his shoulder and thought that looked like fabulous living at its best.

"Or a rapper," Hayden offered. They realized the last two ideas had rhymed, so they came up with mapper, flapper (he does have nice knees), and yapper, which Ted said he'd been training for all his life.

"Be an unemployment counselor who truly understands," Olson said.

"How about a camel caravan conductor?" I said. "You like hot weather."

"Run a lemonade stand," Joshua shouted. To him, this was the ultimate in entrepreneurship.

"I have one for you," Cory said. "New missionary liquidator. You could sell all the stuff the elders leave behind when they get transferred."

"I think you should work at a zoo," Ellie suggested. "You're really good with animals."

"Criminal mastermind!" Hayden said, having recently watched a Batman cartoon.

"Nope," I said. "I have it. Family masseur."

"What's that?" Ellie asked.

"That means he gives all of us back rubs," I said.

Ted rolled his eyes. "Like the time you got whiplash last month."

"What's this?" Olson asked. "You were in a wreck?"

I sighed, a little weary of this story, but the family was urging me to tell it.

"Okay, fine," I said. Then I told him what had happened.

One night I had a horrible dream that I was hit by another car going full speed. I probably dreamed it because I'd been praying for Ted to have an accident, but I did not include that suspicion. At any rate, I was so upset that I sat straight up in bed, woke up, realized it was just a dream, and then lay back down and went to sleep. But in sitting up so fast, I must have pulled my neck and back muscles out. The next morning I had to go visiting teaching (a quick explanation to Olson of what that is), but I could hardly get in the car or turn around to look, and I really didn't think I should be driving. But I got to my first appointment and the woman I was visiting saw the pain I was in and told me to get right over and see her chiropractor. She even called ahead and to tell him I was coming.

I drove right over and they asked me to fill out a form describing my injury. What could I say? I wrote, "I dreamed I was in a car accident." The next thing I knew the doctor himself came into the waiting room and said, "No one has ever written that on one of my forms." And he was looking at me like I was an idiot.

"Stupid dream drivers," Cory interrupted.

"That's right," I agreed.

By now Olson was laughing so hard his eyes were watering, and I held my palms out. "So now you know about Ted's crazy sister."

"It's like Lucy," Olson said. "Only a little bit worse."

"Who's Lucy?" Hayden asked.

"Oh, it's an old actress who's just like your mom," Cory said.

I stared at him.

"Well, you are," he shrugged. "We'll have to rent some DVDs and show the kids."

My list of forbidden funeral anecdotes was growing.

"Last week she went on a date with Dad wearing her bedroom slippers," Hayden said, as if someone had called for further examples of my vanishing intellect.

"What's this?" Ted asked.

"Well, that was totally not my fault," I began.

Cory nodded. "Here we go," he said.

"First of all, we just went out for a quick dish of ice cream," I said. "It was not some big, fancy date."

"Noted," Cory said, pretending to be hurt.

"What did you have?" Olson asked.

"I had a scoop of mango and a scoop of pecan," Cory said.

"I got Chocolate Showers," I said, "which is a rich vanilla filled with dark, milk, and white chocolate shavings."

"Back to the slippers," Ted said.

"We were sitting there at one of those little bistro tables, and a woman walked in, took one look at me, rolled her eyes, and shook her head. Like I'm some robber or something."

"You do look like a robber," Ted said. "Go on."

"I said to Cory, 'That woman just rolled her eyes at me.' Only Cory didn't care. The whole world could roll their eyes at him and he wouldn't give it a second thought."

Now all the adult men high-five each other and agree this was the correct manly reaction to have.

"I would have noticed it too," Ellie said, one vote for womanly sensitivity.

"So now," I continued, "I'm thinking, *I don't even know this woman, so why would she be so rude to me?* And then suddenly I look down and catch a glimpse of my feet. I am wearing fluffy, tiger-striped slippers!"

Hayden and Joshua were cackling over this, enjoying their mother's embarrassment.

"So I said to Cory, 'I'm in my slippers! Quick! We have to get out of here!' and I dashed to the car and jumped in. Cory was acting like there was no rush whatsoever and slowly followed me out, still eating his ice cream."

"Once I get in the car, she starts slapping the heck out of my arm," Cory reported.

"How could he not tell me I was wearing slippers?" I said.

"And how am *I* supposed to notice if *she* hasn't even noticed?" Cory asked the group.

"Are you kidding?" I said. "It is thirty times easier to see other people's feet than your own. They're at an angle from your eyes instead of straight down."

"Statistics again," Cory said.

"But it's true," I said. "It's way easier to see other people's feet. And I would certainly tell you if you were walking out the door in your slippers!"

"So notice this is now *my* fault," Cory said.

"Certainly!" I said. "You should have had your eyes open and done something! No wonder that woman rolled her eyes."

"Because of me," Cory said.

"Well, duh," I said. "There is no way any husband could leave the house without his wife noticing slippers on his feet, and that just goes to show you that wives are helpful and husbands are oblivious."

I turned to the kids. "And if anyone tells that story at my funeral, they're cut out of the will."

"I'M oblivious? Ladies and gentlemen," Cory said, "I would like the records of the court to show—"

"Oh, no you don't," I said. "You are not going to grandstand, like this is your closing argument in some—some case of yours."

Olson was shaking his head. "Marriages are all alike," he muttered. "And the sooner a man learns who's in charge, the happier he'll be." Then he looked up at Ted and Cory. "And it isn't us."

Chapter 11

If I didn't think it would traumatize the kids for life, I'd put up a poster about our dimwit dog. Only instead of a Wanted poster, it would be a Not Wanted poster, and it would feature an 11 x 14 photo of Peanut. It would explain why she is *not* wanted, and would list the accompanying costs of everything she has chewed up or peed on.

But just as I'm envisioning the poster, she curls up in my lap and looks at me with those blasted brown eyes—and she gets to live another day. The kids, of course, think she's the cutest dog ever created—so cute, in fact, that she should have her own show on TV. I support this wholeheartedly, as it would require us to put her on a plane and fly her to Los Angeles, where she would undoubtedly have to live (with someone else) for tapings. But I don't explain that part.

And, deep in my heart, I love animals too. I've always allowed the kids to bring in whatever pets they've fallen in love with, from turtles to goldfish to a screaming cockatiel that could throw birdseed as far as the vacuum cord could reach and that wanted nothing more than to kill the family in cold blood. The only safe one was Ellie, whom he would serenade with every song and sound he had memorized, including the beep of the microwave and the ring of the phone. Unfortunately, he lasted only two years because Ellie sprayed her room with air freshener and that, apparently, does not sit well with birds' lungs.

Ellie's love of animals has led to more than one disappointment. The latest was an incident in her fourth-grade classroom.
Seven Buddhist monks had come over from Tibet to proselyte in
the schools. How they got a grant to do this is anybody's guess—
but there they were, standing there in saffron-colored robes and
sandals and heads shaved bald, telling the assembled fourth-
graders that if they came to Tibet they'd receive food, housing,
and calm spirits. They would also get to play a musical instrument that, according to Ellie, sounded like a vacuum cleaner. You
don't see other religions making similar presentations, but that's
your tax money at work, keeping things politically correct and
filling our children's heads with wondrous new options and possibilities.

Soon came question-and-answer time. Various students raised
their hands to ask the monks about their studies, their clothing,
their favorite foods. And Ellie, of course, raised her hand and
asked, "Are you allowed to have pets?"

Only the monk didn't hear her exactly right. He got only the
short vowel sound of the *e* and thought she said something else.
"Oh, no, we're not allowed to have sex," he replied, and the entire
assembly, teachers included, burst into laughter. Ellie, needless to
say, was mortified.

One might think it couldn't get any worse, but the monk then
continued, wagging his finger and elaborating on why there would
be "none of that," until Ellie was forced to shout, "I said PETS!"

Everyone was still in stitches as the monk just calmly went on
to say there were a few cows wandering about, and maybe a dog
or two. But it was too late to salvage the moment, and the entire
school was red-faced and giggly. Ninety-five percent of them (and
this is a true statistic) hadn't even seen "the film" yet, but in this
day and age, fourth-graders know plenty about sex.

Ellie came home being tormented by every upsetting emotion
known to man. I sympathized completely and resisted telling her
she probably inherited the Lucy gene from me.

Last year there was another animal fiasco in her school. The third-graders had just finished an eight-week project raising steelhead trout, which are actually salmon. After eight weeks, the little wimps were still only an inch long (the fish, not the students). If this were a hatchery, they'd go broke. Nevertheless, it was now time for the big ceremonial releasing of these guppy-sized critters into the local river.

Who got the stinky job of cleaning out the tanks and gravel with Betadine? Me, of course. Who stupidly volunteered to be one of the parent drivers, taking a vanload of kids to the river for the big good-bye? Me again. (Why should I reek alone?)

So here were thirty kids, all dressed in blue plastic ponchos because it was raining like crazy, standing on the banks of the American River. Each poured a little Styrofoam cup of water containing a single fish into the river. In the weeks before this sentimental scene, each kid had to give a trout speech, make a diorama, and write a song. Waaay too much emphasis on fish eggs, if you ask me. I could only imagine what Ted would think if he were part of this.

So now the kids were bidding *adieu,* calling out, "Good-bye, Wiggly," "Good-bye, Steelie! Swim to the ocean!" Yeah, right. What these kids haven't noticed, but which I spotted the second we got there, is that four or five species of birds were circling overhead, swooping down and fishing for their breakfast. A block away, at a bend in the river near our house, were at least two hundred ducks and geese that I knew of personally, including the three screaming marauders who recently graced our backyard. These fish didn't have a chance! They'd be lucky to make it two blocks. Tell me: What is the point of taking eight weeks to make a cookie?

So I hurried the kids along, hoping they wouldn't notice that they were releasing their pets right into the jaws of death. But they were dawdling, enjoying this touchy-feely ceremony. Finally I more or less yanked the kids into my minivan before the feeding frenzy began. A couple of the other parents glared at me like I was rushing a Kodak moment, and I wondered if maybe I should say something about the value of a project that basically raises bait.

I also wondered this: If they're just going to get gobbled up anyway, why didn't we fry them ourselves and have a nice lunch? No wonder people homeschool.

So this whole animal topic brings me back to Peanut, the erstwhile innocent Disney animation of a loveable creature with oversized eyes. Only now she was the fugitive, hiding under the sofa so that only her wet little heart-shaped nose was sticking out when I got back from visiting teaching.

And why, you ask, was she hiding? Because she had *shredded my sheers*. That's right—the sheer curtains that hang under the heavier draperies. Evidently these are made of a material as irresistible to dogs as catnip is to cats. Tiny bite marks were all over the lower two feet of the fabric, where she had clearly jumped to attack these menacing curtains with every fiber of her being. They were covered with tears and snags. Had the curtains actually been alive, they would now surely be dead.

"Peanut—" I growled. I could hear a miniature tail hitting the underside of the sofa. I put down Juliet, who had fallen asleep on the ride home, and the rest of the kids waited to see what terrible fate awaited our smallest canine family member.

"Come out here, Peanut," I ordered. More wagging. Finally I reached under the sofa and pulled her out by the collar. I showed her the curtains. "Did you do this?" I demanded to know, as if she could speak English. It would have made just as much sense to lecture the curtains for not getting out of the way.

"Bad Peanut," I said. "*Bad* Peanut." I know what all the books say; it's useless to spank a dog, so I just let her go, tail between her legs and quivering with guilt. Ellie started toward her. "Uh-uh-uh," I said. "Don't you *dare* reward that dog with affection after what she did."

Ellie stopped. "But she looks so pitiful."

"That's the idea," I said. "She has practiced looking pitiful as a survival skill. And apparently it works, because she should be strapped to an electric chair. Instead she's going to wait twenty minutes and then come dancing out in a pink tutu ready for her next round of applause."

The kids all looked relieved that Peanut had not been thrown through a window (the appropriate healthy response to a vandal) but was instead being allowed to regroup under the dining table, where she could pray that we'd all forget her misdeeds. She, herself, was already in the process of forgetting them this very minute.

"How much do curtains cost?" Ellie whispered as I was tearing up lettuce for a salad.

"You don't even want to know," I said. And I was *so* tempted to add, "Well, there goes our family vacation this year," just to elicit support, but then realized what a cheap shot that would be and just began slicing cucumbers instead.

That night over dinner, after Cory had calmed down about the curtains, the kids told him about our afternoon. I had taken them to a local nursing home to visit a sister whose name was on our ward records but who had never been visited.

Ellie looked somberly at her father. "It was a disaster, Daddy," she said.

"Well, not a total disaster," I said. "At least we found Sister Shumway."

"She had been missing?" Cory asked.

"No, but we had assigned her to a visiting teaching team that never got over there. I thought I'd check out her situation."

"Good for you," Cory said. "Too many of these sweet older sisters fall through the cracks."

"Sweet?!" Hayden burst out.

Cory looked over at me.

"Well," I said, "*sweet* isn't the first word that comes to mind."

"She was a *witch*!" Joshua whispered.

I smiled at our little five-year-old. "She was not a witch," I said, emphasizing every word.

"Well," Joshua said, "she *looked* like a witch. Even the warts!"

"And her nose was hooked," Hayden said.

I smiled at Cory. "Does this sound like a *Monty Python* sketch to you?"

He laughed. "And did she cast a spell on you?" he asked the boys.

"Mom wouldn't let her," Joshua said, as certain of this as he was that the sun would rise tomorrow.

"She was not a witch," I repeated. "She was just old and her hair wasn't combed."

"And she was mean," Ellie added.

"Reaaaally mean," Joshua said.

So now Cory had to hear the whole story. I explained that when we got there, she was yelling at some of the nurses about never taking her anywhere.

"But you went to the mall this morning," one nurse said. "Don't you remember, Vivian?"

She did not. The nurse turned and whispered to me, "It's so frustrating when they can't remember something fun they did. We also had a beach-party-themed lunch, but she popped the ball with her fork and said it was stupid."

Well, the merits of a beach-themed lunch aside, I had to agree that popping the beach ball was out of line.

"Sister Shumway," I said, leaning down to her wheelchair, "I'm Syd and these are my children—Ellie, Hayden, Joshua, and Juliet."

She frowned. "You've got too many kids. What's the matter with you?"

Ah. I stood up and nodded at the nurses. "Maybe we'll take her to the recreation room. I noticed they were setting up for something musical in there."

Then I turned to Sister Shumway. "How does that sound?" I asked. "Would you like to see some entertainment?"

"It's never any good," she snapped.

While other residents were waiting for the show to begin, one of the aides was playing "YMCA" on a boom box and trying to elicit clapping from elderly folks who never liked that song in the first place.

Finally the social director announced that they were going to have an Irish sing-along.

I leaned down to Sister Shumway. "Well, how do you like that!" I said. "A sing-along! That should be fun."

"It won't be," she snarled. The kids were looking at me with *Can we get out of here?* in their eyes.

The social director plugged in a video of a dozen singers in Irish costumes (who, all kidding aside, were way, way, *way* worse than your worst ward dinner entertainment could ever hope to be) and passed out some lyric sheets.

I smiled at the other residents, who looked at me as if I were in worse shape than they were.

"And then it hit me," I said to Cory. "One little detail had been overlooked: IRISH SONGS ARE MOSTLY ABOUT DEATH!"

Cory leaned in. "And nobody caught this."

"Nope," I said. "Naturally it started with 'Danny Boy,' which is a tearful song about a father sending his son off to die in the war, knowing he'll be in his own grave soon. Then there was a morbid little ditty that went, 'She died of a fever and no one could save her and that was the end of sweet Molly Malone.'"

Somehow in the retelling this began to amuse our kids and they started giggling. Ellie even insisted on singing that terrible chorus so Cory could get the full effect. Her brothers only giggled louder.

"So now," I said, "I was stealing sideways glances at everybody to see if anyone had freaked out yet, but so far they were all just mumbling along. And the social director was just clapping her hands and smiling through all these—" I searched for a description—"these tales of imminent demise."

Now the kids were howling.

"And then the third song was about an Irish guy who died working on the railroad," Hayden reported, his eyes watering with laughter.

"So," I said, "I finally told Sister Shumway that maybe we should take her outside for a stroll so she could get some sunshine.

I mean, I couldn't just leave her in there with nothing but death and destruction."

Now Cory was laughing as well. "No, you couldn't."

"But the wheelchair lock was down and I couldn't get it unlocked until they were already singing 'Down Went McGinty,' a clever number about some guy who survived several near-fatal accidents before finally throwing himself into a river."

Now Cory and the kids were laughing so hard that Joshua was almost choking on his glass of milk.

"And people wonder why nursing homes are so depressing," I said. "If they'd just change the music—"

"Yeah, that's it." Cory laughed. "It's all about the music."

"Well, in this case, that might have helped."

"So did she thank you for coming to visit?"

"Oh," I said, getting back to the story. "No, she didn't. In fact, she said she wants nothing to do with the Church and to stop bothering her."

"See?" Joshua said. "A witch!"

Cory laughed. "Well, at the rate her visiting teachers are going, I'd say she's going to get her wish."

Chapter 12

AFTER DINNER I GOT A call from a sister in the ward who was throwing a bridal shower for the Relief Society president's daughter. Only now she wanted to bow out and asked me if I could take over.

"Of course," I said. "Why—what happened?"

"Well, my tree trimmers are coming the next week, and I just don't want to overload my schedule."

Huh? Wait. *The tree trimmers—who require you to do absolutely nothing except write them a check when they're finished—aren't coming until an entire week later, and this would overload your schedule?*

"I'll be happy to have it at my house," I said. And I would love to host a party for Amy; I taught her in Young Women and was thrilled when we got word of her engagement.

But I have to wonder about the sister who had planned to do this and then canceled. It reminds me of Ted teaching me about Christmas lights when I was a teenager. Allow me to explain. There are people who roll with life's punches and ultimately survive the storms; then there are those who flip out because the sky is gray, becoming hysterical knots of panic and requiring bed rest and possibly medication.

It's exactly the same with Christmas lights. On some kinds of lights, the whole strand has a nervous breakdown and fritzes into oblivion if a single bulb burns out. These are called "series" lights. They are like your Aunt Theona, who gets a run in her stockings and has to take a Valium. They are like the multiphobic neurotics in every family and workplace—those who operate on the edge of hysteria and turn every mishap into a colossal catastrophe. *Drama* doesn't even begin to describe it.

The other kind of light strand is called "parallel." These stay lit even if one bulb goes out—and this is obviously the kind of lighting everybody wants. These are the people who quietly change lanes if a semi-truck a couple of blocks ahead pulls into their lane. They continue their conversation and maintain a steady mood, eventually passing the truck with nary a glance. Series people gasp and swerve, break into a nervous sweat, and shout, "Did you see that guy? He just pulled right into my lane! Did you see that?"

It is needless to say that parallel people have lower blood pressure, happier lives, and more organized desks. Series people have worrisome levels of caffeine in their blood, lives of chaos, and desks covered with papers from as far back as 1987. Series people burst into tears over burned dinners, canceled plans, and broken appliances. Parallel people take daily setbacks in stride and simply set about finding the solution.

Parallel people hobble around with sprained ankles while series people lie in bed and worry that their ankle will become arthritic. Parallel people go looking for a job if they get fired. Series people go looking for a bar.

And, like I said, parallel are the strands everybody wants. But wards are filled with a mixture of personalities. This is one reason why being active in the Church helps refine us—we have to learn to get along with every type of light strand, even some that haven't yet been invented.

So when a person gets overwhelmed over something you thought was nothing, just realize you're dealing with a series light strand, and don't try to cajole it into being a parallel one. It is literally in the hard wiring.

Ellie enjoyed helping me plan the shower, and Donna was more than delighted to handdesign every invitation, even though she lives in another ward and doesn't even know Amy or her mother.

I think the highlight was a surprise video we made of Amy's fiancé, Dallin, answering questions such as, "What was the first thing you noticed about Amy?" and "Where did you go on your first date?" We had passed out questionnaires to all the guests, had them fill in their guesses, and then played the video, stopping before each of Dallin's answers to see what Amy would say as well. It gave the guests a fun glimpse into her sweetheart's personality and allowed everyone to laugh when they learned Amy had changed a flat tire for Dallin and he had shown her how to crochet.

We passed around a book for guests to fill with their advice for a happy marriage. I put in my usual, "Buy pets that match your furniture," a tactic that prevents the dreaded dog-hair-on-the-sofa dilemma. But there were some great, serious bits of advice as well, including, "Don't say it. Whatever you're thinking, DON'T SAY IT!" Sounds funny at first, but longtime marrieds can attest to the value of biting one's tongue.

As we were cleaning up after the shower, I thought of a few more things I've learned over the years. Here is my list, should you need a cheat sheet for your next bridal shower:

> 1. After your husband expresses concern about whether a tall crystal vase might get knocked over if it's placed on the family rom coffee table, do not respond with a sentence that begins, "Only a moron . . ."
> 2. Do not ask what your husband is thinking. He is not thinking anything, and your question just points this out.
> 3. Do not scoff at the importance of watching the play-offs before the play-offs for the division championships before the Super Duper Final Series Winners.
> 4. Do not suggest at any point—even if you are approaching the Canadian border—that your

husband stop and ask for directions. Take along some knitting and make a sweater.

5. Do not ask your husband to tell his funny stories when invited to dinner at someone else's home. Similarly, do not ask him to make his funny ducky sounds.

6. Do not volunteer your husband to help the neighbors with household repairs he has claimed to have done but which you have not personally witnessed him doing.

7. Do not throw away the gigantic, 64-ounce soda cups your husband is saving because he gets a discount when he goes in for a refill.

8. Never say, "But we already have a set of tools."

9. Never ask, "Notice anything different about me?"

10. Never ask, "Does this make me look fat?"

11. Do not make soy burgers.

12. Do not refer to your husband's shirts as "tops."

13. Do not tell the story about your husband that his mother told you—you know, the one about the time he wet the bed at camp.

14. Do not surprise your husband by signing up for a different phone service, insurance company, Internet provider, or bank, even if the ad sounds irresistible.

15. If your husband is out with a male friend somewhere, do not tell callers, "He's with his boyfriend."

16. Do not invite your husband to babysit your sister's kids with you for the weekend so that he can see what it's like to be a parent.

17. Do not point out the remaining nuts and bolts of a kit your husband has just finished assembling.

18. Do not try to change your husband. It won't

work, it will tick him off, and it will remind him of his mother—not exactly the makings of a romantic mood.

19. Do not say, "Oh, look, you missed one," when your husband is holding a leaf blower and has been cleaning up the yard for thirty minutes.

20. Do not compare your husband's work to the handyman's. Just let it go and be glad he agreed to hire a handyman.

This brings me to an interesting exception. How do you feel about hiring Church members? It's a conundrum, you realize. We want to help one another and we certainly like the idea that our money will be tithed by the recipient. On the other hand, we relinquish the ability to complain about shoddy workmanship or unfulfilled promises, don't we? It's hard to become the demanding customer, even when the person has let us down, because we don't want to create hard feelings.

I leave this decision to you, but I will give you this definite advice: Never hire a bipolar handyman, LDS or not. I like crazy people as much as the next person (more, if you ask Cory), but you are in for a load of misery if you hire someone who needs to be on medication and who is not.

Next to choosing the correct spouse, this one decision can account for 90 percent of your future happiness. Okay, I made that statistic up, but it's pretty important. Take, for example, Barney. We hired Barney because he was an inactive member and we thought we could help him find his way back. But Barney can drive you crazy in five seconds or less—faster than many Porsches can hit sixty miles an hour.

If he is in a jovial mood, you will mistakenly think everything is going to go well. But there is a huge difference between cheerful and hysterically ecstatic. If you get trapped in a small bathroom while he is loudly extolling the virtues of, say, shower grout, you can go deaf. Your husband can emerge from this encounter staggering down the hall, wiping spit from his face, and grabbing for something to steady himself.

Laughter beyond any level you have ever heard can echo through your attic and smack into your kitchen, making you bang your head on the underside of the sink. When you go to the attic to investigate what on earth could be so funny, you find that it is nothing.

And in this fit of euphoria, the bipolar handyman will go easy on himself and forgive a little quarter-of-an-inch here and there. The next thing you know, you will be tripping over your own floor. Your faucet handles will turn backward and your stove won't fit its intended space—all because someone was thinking happy little thoughts instead of measuring accurate little measurements.

If Barney is in a bad mood, he comes over; drops his tools, ladder, and buckets wherever he happens to be (in the doorway, say); and begins yelling about government corruption, cowardly police who won't arrest his neighbors, and rich celebrities who give nothing back. Your own neighbors will crane their necks to see who's about to kill somebody, and you'll have to yank Barney into the house and slam the door.

His work will be disastrous. He will emit loud, gaseous noises and will swear like a bipolar handyman. You will wait as long as possible, and finally you will drive like a demon to Nordstrom's— where you will buy three new outfits, complete with a chocolate malt on your way home. And you'll have to hang your new outfits in a crooked closet.

So now you have plenty of advice for a happy marriage *and* a home that is not shaped like a rhombus.

But I still like the idea of trying to reactivate people, by whatever means necessary. Take Ted, for example. I am up for whatever creative methods it might take. I just don't advise hiring bipolar handymen.

Annie called to compliment me on the fun shower and to tell me she had just joined a gym. "But you have to come with me the first time," she said. "You know all about exercise and can show me what to do."

"Are you kidding? I just run. I know nothing about that fancy equipment."

"Come with me anyway," she begged. "I don't want to go to a spinning class all by myself."

Okay, fine. I had been wondering what those classes were like, anyway, so I agreed to meet her on Tuesday evening after dinner, when Cory could watch the kids.

Let me just ask something. DO YOU HAVE ANY IDEA HOW HARD THOSE SEATS ARE? Within ten minutes I had bruised myself beyond recognition. Not that anyone in particular would be called in to do the recognizing. I couldn't believe there was an entire class, pedaling away, oblivious to what had to be dozens of RUINED BACK ENDS. This was nothing but birth control put to a catchy beat.

"You have to get used to it," the instructor said when I staggered away from the bike, wincing in pain.

Then what's the point? I guess you could get used to hitting yourself in the head with a hammer too, but why would you do that? On top of everything else, the instructor kept yelling "Push!" into the microphone, which only served to remind me of being in hard labor, so *that* was just lovely. Obviously that woman had never given birth.

Annie was laughing at me so hard that she fell off her bike and hit her shin on the bike bar; they had to pack it with ice. We finally limped out of there together, got in her car, and decided to stop for some greasy tacos. It was the only thing left to do, the way we saw it.

When she dropped me off and I walked into my house, there on the carpet was an entire map of the world, thrown up entirely by Peanut. While I was gone the family thought they'd let her have some of the sloppy joes they were eating, and *voila!* Art!

"Have you people seen this?" I shouted to the rest of them, who were in the family room watching a movie and had no idea of the havoc that had been wreaked right under their noses.

"Eww," Ellie said, echoed by her brothers.

I stared at the disaster. All the continents were represented, even the boot of Italy and the Aleutian Islands.

"We ought to take a picture and get her on *The Tonight Show* with Jay Leno," Cory said.

"That idiot should get an Eagle Scout award for making a giant world map," I said. "If only she could have done it on a playground."

"It's like she's a genius," Hayden said.

"An evil genius," I muttered as I came back with carpet cleaner and a giant roll of paper towels. "You all get to help," I said, tearing off lengths of paper towel for everyone.

"What? But that's the mom's job," Hayden resisted.

"I'm not the one who gave her sloppy joes to eat," I said, casting a glance at Cory, the adult on the scene who let this happen. "Besides, I have a ruined back end."

The kids all stared at me. "A *what*?"

"Never mind," I grumbled.

The phone rang and Cory took my paper towels from me, letting me off cleanup duty long enough to answer it.

It was Liza Carlton. I thanked her for calling just in time to get me out of yet another disaster-control moment. Then I told her about my bruised bottom.

"Okay, I can top you," she said. "Last Sunday, in bishop's council meeting, I discovered that I am on the brink of hag-dom."

"What?" I laughed.

"It's true. In four and a half years I will officially pass my expiration date and become a hag."

I had to hear what on earth had happened. Evidently the young Relief Society president in Liza's ward had said that there were a number of older widows who wanted to feed the missionaries but couldn't, since they didn't have a priesthood holder in the home.

So one of the missionaries piped up that in his last area the rule was that after age fifty-five, a sister could have the elders in her home as long as another elderly sister was there as well.

"Do you realize what this means?" Liza said. "This means that in four more years I will no longer be recognizable as a woman. I will have lost all appeal."

Now I was laughing hysterically. "Hey, I'm coming up right behind you," I said.

"Yeah, right." Liza snarled. "I've got to get older friends. You have no idea what it's like to stare hag-dom in the face."

"You are not a hag," I laughed.

"Not yet," she snapped. "But soon. We'll see if a fruit basket lands on my porch this Christmas. And if it does, I'm getting out my Glock."

By now the kids were traipsing by me with disgusting wads of paper towels, so I had to hang up and join the cleanup of what was now an even bigger mess, as if such a thing was possible. But at least I'd had a break from disaster with Liza's latest adventure.

Or so I thought. As soon as I hung up, the phone rang again. It was Ted. Only this time, he was calling from an ambulance.

Chapter 13

"THEY'RE SAYING MY COLLARBONE IS probably broken," he said as matter-of-factly as if a repairman had just told him his lawn mower needed a new belt.

"What?" I asked. "How did this happen?"

"My brakes went out," he said. "It's rush hour too, so it's amazing that I rolled the truck without hitting anyone."

"What? You rolled it?" My heart was pounding.

"Yeah, it's pretty totaled. But I'm fine, really." I could hear the medics talking in the background. By now, Cory and the kids had overheard enough to stop in their tracks and listen.

"They're taking me to UC Davis," Ted continued—meaning the medical center, not the university.

"I'll be right there," I said. I hung up and turned to my family. "Ted's been in a car accident," I said. "He's on his way to the hospital. I'm going to meet him there."

"Should we come?" Cory asked.

"No, this is my doing," I said. "I prayed him there, and I ought to be the one who shows up."

Now the kids were beyond shocked. They turned to Cory, whose eyes were closed as he tried to summon patience. "Yes," he said, after taking a huge breath. "Your mother prayed for Uncle Ted to have some kind of accident."

I didn't stay to hear the rest of the discussion; I knew Cory would explain my desperate attempts to save Ted from eternal doom. And if it involved some broken bones, that was a small price to pay for exaltation.

Nevertheless, I prayed as I drove, hoping God would teach him through this experience and that his injuries wouldn't be serious.

I flew into the emergency parking lot, slammed on my brakes, and dashed into the waiting room, where they let me in to see Ted right away. He was on a gurney with his arm in a sling.

"Why don't you have ice on that?" I asked.

He tried to shrug and then winced. "They haven't put any ice on it," he said.

I whirled around, furious. "What's the matter with you people?" I shouted. "Don't you put ice on injuries anymore?"

No one appeared to be listening, so I marched up to a nurse's station. "This man needs ice," I demanded. It was not a missionary moment, but I didn't care. Finally one nurse slowly scooted her chair out and said she'd take a look at it.

"Could you possibly move more slowly?" I snapped. "I'm sure it's swollen up by now!" I shook my head in exasperation and glared at anyone who glanced my way. Finally the nurse returned with a cold pack.

"And why is he in this sling?" I asked. "If it's his collarbone—"

"This is standard," the woman snapped back at me.

"Well then raise your standards, honey!" I was sort of—okay, not sort of—I was extremely shocked at the tone coming out of my mouth, but I was also running on total adrenaline and had precisely no patience for inept workers. I may not be a nurse or a doctor, but basic first-aid training wasn't even evident.

"Have you taken an Xray?" I asked.

"Not yet."

"Not yet? What are you waiting for? How can you possibly treat this man if you don't even know the extent of his injuries?"

Right about then was when I realized Ted had been saying my name over and over, louder each time, in an effort to calm me down. "I'm fine," he finally said. "It's okay; they'll get to it."

I ignored him and turned back to the nurses. "Do you really need me to come in here and tell you how to handle an emergency?" I was addressing three of them now, and not one of them was very happy about it. "Snap into action!" I yelled. "Pretend this is an EMERGENCY room—hello?"

Now they were glaring at me. The oldest of the three said I should wait outside.

"How about *you* wait outside?" I barked. "You're certainly useless in here."

Now Ted was raising himself up on his bed and glancing at the nurses to assure them he would muzzle me himself. In the meantime, a doctor was being summoned to quiet down the hysterical woman with the collarbone guy.

"We're going to have to ask you to leave," the doctor said.

"Oh, please," I rejoined. "Like I'm the most unruly person you've ever had in here. You simply don't like having your mistakes pointed out. This man needs attention and you guys are . . . are chewing gum and . . . and waddling around like this is a . . . a morgue or something."

I could now feel the tension building in the very air around the doctors and nurses, but I couldn't seem to stop myself. Maybe it's because I knew I was responsible for Ted being there in the first place.

Ted was standing now and trying to pull me to a chair with his one good arm. "It's going to be fine, Syd," he was saying.

I allowed him to sit me down beside the gurney, which he then got back on.

"Have you even given him anything for the pain?" I snarled.

"A doctor needs to order that," one of the nurses said.

I wanted to say, *And I commend you for your patience with a truly ill-tempered woman* (me), but I could not make the words come out. "And how long before a doctor wanders by to order pain meds?" I said instead.

"We're taking care of it," said another nurse who was a little testy but certainly more composed than I was.

And now, I admit with great embarrassment, I did something I have never done before. I took my hand and pointed at my eyes with two fingers, then back at the nurses with the same two. "I'm watching you," I said. Slowly, and with much eye rolling, the nurses walked away and went about their work.

Ted was staring at the ceiling. "Did I ever tell you that you remind me of Mother Theresa?"

"Oh, shut up, Ted," I said. "Someone's got to advocate for you. These people are bumblers. Bunglers. Bundle—bungle—"

He sighed. "Burglars, perhaps?"

I looked him in the face, took a big breath, and then exhaled.

"Feeling a little calmed down?" he asked.

I nodded and glanced at the slow-motion emergency room. "Somewhat."

"Good."

I looked over at him again. "You know I prayed you in here."

"Yep."

"You knew that?"

"I figured it."

And then the tears came, flowing down my cheeks and dropping sloppily off my chin. "I'm so sorry," I said.

"I know you want me to have some life-changing experience," he said. "And I know you've probably prayed for far worse than this."

"No, honestly," I said. "This is the worst that I've prayed for. I promise."

Now he chuckled. "Do you realize how this sounds? That you're praying for all these horrible experiences?"

"I know," I said. "But I'm just desperate! I can hardly breathe sometimes, Ted. I get so upset thinking about you not being active in church—"

Now he shook his head. "Syd, you are crazy. Did you pray for me to lose my job too?"

"No! Are you kidding? How could you think such a thing?"

"Let's see," Ted said. "You prayed for me to roll my truck and end up in the hospital, but you're offended that I should think you would pray for me to lose my job."

"Well, you need a job," I said.

"I also need a truck. And a collarbone."

"I didn't want it to be a serious accident," I said. "Just one that would make you realize how precious life is and how short it can be."

Ted groaned and shifted his weight on the gurney. "Well, message received. I do think God was protecting the people around me. I mean, if you knew how crowded that freeway was, it was a pure miracle that someone else didn't get hit."

I sniffled and wiped tears off my cheeks. "And you have to realize God was watching over you too," I said. "I mean, think how much worse it could have been."

"Especially with you praying for it," Ted said. "By the way, thanks a lot."

I put my hand on his good shoulder. "I really am sorry," I said.

"The truck is totaled."

I stared into my lap and apologized again. "Do you think your insurance will cover it?"

"Hope so. We'll see."

"You're reacting kind of . . . calmly about all this."

"Well," he said, "Someone has to keep a cool head. Obviously it won't be you . . . "

"I just—I just feel so responsible," I said. "And I love you. I can't stand to watch people who should be bustling about, helping you—"

"I know," he said. "I knew the minute I came in here that you weren't gonna like it."

I smiled. "It's not my speed," I admitted. And then, finally, they came to Xray Ted and give him some medication. By then I was under a bit more control, so you will be happy to know that I resisted saying, *Well, finally! Hallelujah!* Instead, I waited (quietly!), and within an hour Ted was released to go home. They don't put casts on collarbones, and there wasn't much more they felt they could do.

"Thank you," I muttered as we left. "And I'm sorry I, uh, sort of chewed you all out." Most of the nurses just ignored me; a couple of them smirked.

Ted was given instructions for showering and general advice about "no heavy lifting," as if he'd want to increase his pain by doing that. Within a couple of days I drove him to see the totaled truck and retrieve some CDs under the seat that had survived the tumble across five lanes. Ted then began the long process of dealing with insurance to get another vehicle.

I offered to nurse him back to health by having him stay at our house, but he just laughed and shook his head. "You'd nurse me to death," he said. "I can't take that much attention."

Within a couple of weeks he was feeling healed enough to join us at a birthday gathering for my dad at our parents' house. He said that, except for twisting in certain directions, he was sure he'd be able to nail down some roofing tiles that were dangling off the side of their house.

"Can't keep a good man down," Cory said, catching himself just before slapping Ted on the back.

Mom kept patting him and saying, "You look so good, Ted." She was clearly relieved to see him up and about.

Cory had explained my prayer to the kids. In doing so, he had tried to teach them that nothing is more important than family— and that being sealed for eternity was the entire point of life. It seemed to sink in, but they were still somewhat appalled at the lengths I would go to just to get Uncle Ted back. "Well," Cory had said, "it shows you how important it is." Thankfully he left off the remaining sentiment—*and it shows you how crazy your mom is.*

But I want you to know I was actually right when I was storming around that emergency room—a month later I learned about a different sling entirely that Ted should have been given that would have aligned his collarbone properly. So you see? They *were* bunglers, after all.

Chapter 14

A COUPLE OF WEEKS LATER I got a call—obviously a recording—from a man who said he was from Frog Prevention.

"Frog Prevention?" I mumbled. "Why would anyone want to prevent frogs?" But I heard something about Southwest Airlines, so I listened. Was there a frog invasion on Southwest? Like *Snakes on a Plane,* only frogs? So then I got to thinking, and realized he had said *fraud* prevention. Good grief—why can't people enunciate? Our Visa card gives us frequent flyer miles on Southwest—so I, the master detective, put this together and called Cory to determine if someone else was using our credit card.

Sure enough, some idiot tried to charge TWENTY-ONE THOUSAND DOLLARS on our card. And get this—he was trying to do this at a Christian bookstore! What on earth could cost twenty-one thousand dollars in there—the entire inventory? Ellie said maybe he was buying artwork. But if you're a crook, why would you want religious artwork? Isn't that a bit hypocritical—like trying to pay your tithing with Monopoly money?

"Well, I'm just glad it wasn't something about preventing frogs," Ellie said when the whole issue was wrapped up.

"Me too," I said. I've always liked frogs. Maybe it's because of Ted and his uncanny ability to help the kids catch them. I remembered catching them with him when I was a little girl, unaware at the time that the last thing most eighteen-year-old guys want to do is take their little sister frogging. We'd spend hours on the muddy banks and Ted would ask me all about my life—my friends, my teachers, my dreams for the future. I took for granted that my future would include Ted at my wedding, a household of little mini-Teds at Christmas, and a darling sister-in-law who saw all the things in him that I did. How I wished he would ask me my dreams today.

I called Mom and suggested we go to lunch. We try to do this every month or so, in addition to occasional Sunday dinners at the farmhouse. This time I thought I'd talk to her about Ted. Obviously the accident didn't have the desired effect on him, so I thought I'd see how she copes with year after year of hoping and waiting. I figured she might also have some ideas.

"We've got to do something," I said. "Chad and Neal are in Colorado and Missouri, so they can't really do much more than phone now and then, and I know he's sick of hearing about it from me . . ."

"I think it's wonderful that you stay close to Ted," Mom said. "I think I've worn him out with my nagging about it. They say all you can do is just love them. Keep their names in the temple, fast for them . . ." She shrugged.

"How can you stand it?" I asked her. "Doesn't it just break your heart every single day?"

She nodded, her eyes tearing up.

"I'm sorry," I said. "I didn't mean to rub salt in the wound—"

"I cry every day," Mom said. "I kneel down to pray for him, and sometimes I feel too weak to get up again. I don't know why the Lord is making us wait so long."

"Well, it's Ted, not the Lord," I said. "He's so stubborn. It seems to me that he's still rebelling."

Mom shook her head. "He's more stubborn than your father." Then she smiled. "And that's saying something."

Dad was known far and wide for his stubbornness. Even my grandparents used to call him *Mule* now and then.

Mom sipped her 7-Up. "Ted came over a week or so before the accident and still referred to us as the 'ScholarshipKeeper' family."

"Oh, geez, how old is that?"

"I know," she said. "But it still smarts. He still feels—I don't know— jealous of you other kids, resentment of Dad and me. Who knows?"

"He's missing his chance to marry and have kids."

"I know. I'm afraid he's going to end up awfully unhappy."

"Why doesn't his bishop go over there and drag him to priesthood meeting?"

Mom smiled. "If only it were that simple. Finding sheep is not quite the same as finding people. You can pick up a sheep and bring back to the herd. But a person has his agency, and you have to *coax* him back. It's much harder."

"Well he's still a lost sheep who deserves some attention," I said.

"How do we know his ward isn't working on it?" Mom said. "Maybe they are and the problem is Ted."

I sighed and picked at my cobb salad.

After a minute, Mom said, "I still blame myself."

"Are you kidding? You were the perfect mother."

She smiled. "Maybe that was the problem. I think I conveyed to you kids that we all had to be perfect. Looking back, I'd do it differently. I'd make room for Ted." And then she stopped, her voice caught in her throat. Tears rolled down her cheeks.

I put my hand on her arm. "I'm sorry, Mom. I really didn't mean to dredge up all these feelings over lunch."

"No, it's fine," she said. "They're right under the surface, anyway. Just don't copy what I did."

"Mom, are you kidding? I want to be exactly like you!"

She shook her head and dabbed at her eyes beneath her glasses. "I pushed too hard."

"But the rest of us turned out okay," I said. "Do you really regret how you raised us?"

She took a breath and tried to collect her emotions. "I do," she said. "There's more to life than achievement and image. I think I even put it ahead of gaining a testimony. And now"—she suddenly looked so old and frail to me—"I'd give anything if Ted had a testimony."

I started crying too, then scooted over in the booth and put my head on her shoulder. "So would I," I said.

Then I pulled back. "But it's not your fault, Mom. Ted knows what's right. In his heart, I believe he knows the Church is true."

"I hope so," she whispered. "I just wish he could remember that."

I came away from our lunch saddened that we couldn't come up with a solution—and maybe even sadder to think that my mother blamed herself every day. It made me want more than ever to help Ted find his way home, if only to ease my mother's heart.

So it was with a discouraged spirit that I went to church that Sunday. As the meeting began, I heard the bishop announce a ward fast for a young man who had been in a motorcycle accident and was going to lose one of his arms.

A wave of sympathy swept over the congregation and crowds of caring members swarmed around the tearful family, who tried bravely to face what was being described as a tragedy. All day people rallied, filling the sign-up sheet for meals and writing notes of encouragement.

I drummed my fingers on the hymnbook I was holding during Sunday School. Cory looked over at me and mouthed, "What's wrong?" but the class had started so I just whispered, "Later."

After church there was a flurry of activity getting ready for dinner, since we had invited some neighbors over. As soon as our neighbors left, our home teacher popped by, then it was time for baths and bed for the kids. By the time I finally got to talk with Cory, we were already in bed.

"Okay, what's up?" he asked. "You seemed on edge all day."

"I think I'm jealous of the Hansens."

"What? The ones with the son—"

I turned to Cory. "Look at the situation from an eternal perspective," I said. "That kid has always been outstanding. He was great in Primary, got so many Scout badges he looked like a Christmas tree, got his Eagle, and you know he's going to go on a mission, get married in the temple, and probably be a bishop one day."

"And?"

"So shoot me for thinking this does not require a ward fast."

"Syd, are you kidding? The boy is losing his arm!"

"Cory, I would give anything in this world, including my own life, if Ted could simply lose an arm but gain eternal life. People don't know what a real tragedy is, Cory."

He thought for a moment. "You'd trade them?"

"In a heartbeat. And you know what? I think I'm angry."

Cory turned to me, started to say something, and then just listened instead.

I continued. "I'm angry because we're always fasting for someone whose future isn't even at risk. We never fast for someone who's been excommunicated or someone who's addicted or someone who has simply lost his way, like Ted. But their situations are far more critical. It's not fair, Cory."

Cory smoothed my hair then pulled me close. "Would you have the ward *not* fast for the Hansen kid?"

I sighed. "No. I think it's right to fast for him. Of course everyone wants the surgery to go well. I just wish Ted's ward would have a fast for him too. I feel like he's slipped through the cracks and nobody cares."

Cory kissed the top of my head. "Why don't you call Ted's bishop and suggest it?"

"They probably don't even know who he is."

We held each other in the darkness for a few minutes. "Why do we only fast for physical problems instead of spiritual problems?" I asked.

"I don't know," Cory said. "Maybe the spiritual ones seem more private, like the person doesn't want it to be everybody's business."

"Oh, please," I said. "Like it's a secret when someone stops coming to church."

"Maybe it's because the spiritual problems go on for so long," Cory said, "whereas physical problems come up suddenly and dramatically. Usually serious physical problems represent a life-or-death situation."

"And what about people who are walking around spiritually dead already? Have we given up on them?" I fought back the tears. "And aren't there a whole lot of things worse than physical death?"

"There are," Cory agreed. "Maybe we need to broaden the way we see emergencies."

I nodded. "And I need to stop being jealous. I think I went in there already discouraged after my lunch with Mom. And discouragement is one of Satan's favorite tools, so there I was, an easy target."

"And now he has you angry, jealous, feeling sorry for yourself, and—what else?" Cory asked.

"That pretty much sums it up. Could I have a blessing?"

Cory hugged me. "Absolutely. I should have thought of that sooner."

We got out of bed and I sat in a straight chair under the bedroom window. Creamy moonlight was pouring in and Italian cypress trees were silhouetted against it. The blessing was beautiful. It filled me with warmth and hope and centered me again on gratitude for my blessings, something always missing when I start feeling sorry for myself.

I got back into bed almost refreshed enough to get up. "Thank you, honey," I said. And then I couldn't help it. "Ted needs to be able to do this," I said.

Cory kissed me. "I know," he said. "And one day he will. Don't give up."

Chapter 15

MONDAY MORNING AS I WAS driving the kids to school, Ellie asked, "How come they say Sunday is a day of rest, when yesterday was one of our busiest days ever?"

I laughed. "That sounds contradictory, doesn't it?"

We stopped to define *contradictory* for the littler ones, then I answered Ellie's question. "Sunday is a day of rest," I said, "but not *rest* the way most people think of it. *Rest* in this sense actually means to depart from your usual activities. It doesn't mean lie down and sleep. It simply means to set aside your routine."

"Okay," Ellie said. "But doesn't that mean to slow down?"

"Well, it can actually mean you speed up," I said. "On the Sabbath we rest from our own work and play, and we do the Lord's work instead. Sometimes it's the very busiest day, and probably should be."

Hayden was moaning. "I thought it was a day when we could just take a nap."

"Surprise," I said, wiggling my eyebrows.

Joshua had found a map under the seat and was pretending to read it. "Go left, then right," he said. "*Left* means toward the turtle tanks, and *right* means toward the bulletin boards."

"What?" I said. He explained that this was how they were teaching left and right in his kindergarten class. I smiled to think that this would still come to mind for him when he was an adult, on those rare occasions when he got turned around and had to remind himself which way was left and right. It's like the occasional thought of bunny ears when we tie our shoes—it never goes away.

And then it hit me—this could be what brings Ted back: He has known the gospel from the time he was a little boy. It's in there. He just needs to recall it.

Actually, he's known it since he was a spirit in the premortal world. Bringing it back to mind is one of the purposes of life.

Now Joshua was making up street names. "Ellie Avenue," he said. "Mommy Lane."

It reminded me of the time we were visiting Chad in St. Louis, and I was navigating for Cory in our rental car. When I mumbled, "Highway 270," Ellie shouted from the backseat, "You weigh 270?!" (This is how rumors get started.)

"No, I do not," I said. "I said *highway*, not *I weigh*!"

Cory was laughing, his face reddening.

"And do you think if I weighed 270 pounds I would be announcing it?" I asked her.

Ellie shrugged.

We pulled up at the school and the kids all kissed Juliet good-bye. This was such a sweet tradition, and I tried not to picture the upcoming reality of their fury when she was old enough to take their toys, knock over their block castles, and spill paint on their homework.

But again, I thought about laying the foundation of caring and love. If they could weld those tender feelings to their hearts, then when childhood spats subsided, that affection might come around again. I watched Chad and Neal quarrel like sworn enemies for several years, but today they have each other's backs and talk on the phone several times a week.

Speaking of the phone, it was ringing when I got back to the house. I picked it up and learned there had been another death in the ward. This time it was the sacrament meeting chorister, Sister Dunfee.

Sister Dunfee was probably a little bit nicer than Sister Shumway in the rest home, but she was not well liked. She would sit up on the stand and look back and forth at the congregation like an oscillating fan, glaring at families with noisy babies. It felt a bit like the searchlight in a prison yard as she scanned us for anyone out of line.

And she'd stop the congregational hymn at random times to chastise us for not breathing in the right place or for not starting the song in unison.

"It's not a choir," Annie whispered to me once.

I try to give the prickly pears the benefit of the doubt. I mean, if the statistics are right (and, of course, I can't recall the real ones, or I'd share them with you), then a certain percentage of every congregation has some baggage we'd rather not think about. I mean, like it or not, you find abuse everywhere (ask any bishop). So maybe she had some pent-up hostility for some reason going back to her childhood. Or maybe she had a personality disorder and her meds weren't working. At least I try to justify the occasional wingnut you find in every ward.

But Sister Dunfee made it difficult. She stood in front of the Relief Society teachers at the end of every lesson, giving them a critique on their delivery, their control of the classroom, their subject matter, and whether they strayed from the manual at any moment. It got to the point that the Relief Society president assigned one of us every month to run interference. We actually had meetings about this! We would either pull Sister Dunfee aside to ask her a question that didn't sound contrived (we hoped), or compliment her on her dress, or ask her to take a meal to somebody. Our other strategy was to put our arm around the teacher and lead her away from Sister Dunfee, like someone blocking a football tackle. Good grief—we almost wrote *X*s and *O*s on a chalkboard like a coach planning out a game.

Twice the sisters she was assigned to visit teach called and begged for a different, less critical teacher. One said that Sister

Dunfee had asked to use the bathroom, then came out and told her how to fold her towels and clean her mirror.

And most of the kids were afraid of her. Although I will say that one time when she was asked to talk about her pioneer heritage in Primary, it was the only moment of absolute silence that room had ever experienced.

Sister Dunfee had never married or had children, but she had a nephew and some nieces who wanted us very involved in the funeral service. They asked our bishop to speak; after his remarks, each of them wanted to share a few memories about her.

"I've got to hear this," Cory said. It's a rare moment when Cory finds fault with someone—so if Cory couldn't wait to hear a kind word about her, you can imagine the sort of person she was.

The food requirements for Sister Dunfee's funeral were not as grand as they usually are for a well-known or popular person, but we nevertheless had plenty of funeral potatoes, ham and other cold cuts, rolls, green salad, and brownies.

More people came than I expected. I whispered to Cory, "I hope they're not all here out of curiosity, like you are."

"Hey, it's one way to get a great showing at your funeral."

That's yet *another* reason I do *not* want a funeral. I will not have people showing up just to see what astonishing stories get told.

As we walked in, I noticed a group of scruffy teenage boys off to one side. Three of them had large gold earrings in both ears. "Sheesh," I whispered to Cory. "The pallbearers look like out-of-work pirates."

"The worst kind," he smiled, whispering back.

The bishop spoke first and gave a beautiful explanation of the purpose of life, the transition to the next life, and how comforting it is to know the plan of salvation.

Then, one by one, her nieces and nephews stood at the podium and spoke. And I was flabbergasted. They honestly *loved* her. The crotchety, overbearing woman I knew wasn't that way at all when she was younger.

One niece told of the time Sister Dunfee had asked the mayor to allow her to plant daffodils all around a poor section of town, just to delight the downtrodden and surprise the children. She spent hundreds of dollars on daffodil bulbs—an even greater fortune back then—just to bring smiles to people she didn't even know.

Another time she threw a giant Thanksgiving feast for everyone on her block—*everyone*! She wanted to make sure no one was forgotten or lonely.

And then her nephew told about her sad life—how she had accumulated china and linens in a trousseau, hoping to marry one day, but the right man never came along. So, one by one, she gave her treasures away to her nieces and nephews.

Every year she volunteered at the high school to help kids enter the speech festival, and she coached several state winners. "I'll bet she's tried to coach one or two of you," her nephew said, smiling. "She honestly was only trying to help."

And then I cried. I couldn't help it; I could feel my eyes burning and the tears tumbled down my cheeks. All this time I was thinking only how obnoxious she was, never stopping to determine her *motive.* Was it to belittle and condemn us? No; she was honestly trying to help us improve. Were her methods unorthodox? Yes, but she wasn't intentionally cruel; she had probably never picked up adequate social skills and had no idea how to approach someone properly.

"In college she was offered a position with an opera company," the nephew went on, "but she turned it down to nurse her mother, whose health was failing. If she seemed a little persnickety about music, it's only because she really was a true musician and wanted the best from everyone around her."

On and on they went, talking about the very quirks I had resented for years, but explaining them all and shedding new light on each one. How I wish I had known these things earlier. And how I wish I had taken the trouble to really get to know

Sister Dunfee and find out why she was like that. I felt terribly unforgiving and ashamed.

After the funeral I thanked the nieces and nephews for sharing their aunt with us, and I honestly meant it. I felt truly grateful to have attended that day and vowed not to judge and dismiss someone like that again.

That Sunday the bishop asked me to come in to his office after sacrament meeting. Well, of course, I was on pins and needles the whole time—was I being released? Would I receive a new calling?

And, of course, those were the first questions I hit him with when I sat down.

"Yes and no," he said, smiling. "You are not being released, but I do want to give you a new calling."

My eyebrows rose.

"I need you to be the ward camp director for girls' camp."

Girls' camp was in a week, so I said, "The one next year, right?"

He smiled. "No. This one."

"WHAAAT?" Weren't there a few months required to get everything organized, gather tents and sleeping bags, practice a skit, and learn how to work one of those portable stove thingies?

"I know it's sudden," he said. "But our regular camp director just got a new job and can't take any time off. I know you'll do a great job with this."

Okay, I have never turned down a calling, but this was ridiculous. "You're joking, right? Cory put you up to this."

"Nope," he said. "I'm serious. And I know you can do it."

"Are you aware that I don't camp?"

"That's okay; I really want a spiritual leader for the girls, not just someone who likes to camp."

"So . . . could I just drive in every day and share a spiritual thought?"

He laughed. "That's not how it works. Talk to Sister Thayne and she'll explain everything to you."

I wanted to refuse. The words ABSOLUTELY NOT were already formed and ready to spit out, but something tingled in my chest and I had a sinking feeling this was an actual calling from the Lord that I needed to accept.

I was blanched and wide-eyed as I came out of the office, and Cory whispered, "What happened?" The kids were all clamoring to know as well, so I pulled them aside and gave them the news.

"YOU?" Cory asked, as stunned as I was.

The kids were laughing their heads off, which tells you how well-known I am for not roughing it.

"But you'll be perfect with the girls," Cory said. "If you survive. I mean, of course you'll survive. What I'm trying to say—" I held up my hand. "Stop. You are making matters worse." I tried to fight the smile that was creeping onto my face, but finally gave in. I honestly wondered if I was dreaming. Or, rather, having a nightmare.

"You hate camping," Hayden whispered.

"I know," I whispered back. "But somehow I have to do this. No kind deed is ever wasted."

Cory was grinning. "I thought it was 'no kind deed ever goes unpunished.'"

"You're not helping," I said, scooting the kids along to class.

"Hey," Ellie said as we headed to the Primary room, "you can take that suitcase made out of church walls."

I laughed. She had to mean the one made from rough, nubby tweed, not unlike the bottom half of the walls in most meetinghouses. And was that a stroke of brilliance, or what, to cover the "toddler handprint section" of the walls with a texture that couldn't show fingerprints?

My first priority the next day was to get together with Sister Thayne and find out what I'd gotten myself into.

And it was SO much worse than I'd thought. Not only would we be sleeping in tents, something I have never been able to do— sleep on a nonbed, that is—but we would be using outhouses, getting water from a faucet attached to a pipe to brush our teeth, and hiking half a mile to the various workshop stations and the eating area. Mosquitoes would abound, showers would be either blistering hot or freezing cold, and there would be an optional three-day hike that would earn me an extra pin.

"A pin?" I laughed. "You're joking, right?"

She was not joking.

"Okay," I said. "I would not hike into the woods to dig a hole for a restroom and to sleep on the rocky soil for a thousand dollars, much less for a measly pin."

She didn't care for my attitude. I sighed. The one thing that sounded almost appealing was that I needed to provide daily messages and gifts as a surprise for each of the girls. This was more like it; something clever and artsy that Donna could help me with. I could see it now: Red glass beads glued on a 3 x 5 card with the scripture about virtuous women being like rubies, a little plastic compass and a quote about letting the Lord be your guide—

"Oh—and you need to read them a story every night, so bring along some books."

Books. Check.

"And you need to give them candy almost constantly, so bring bags of sour balls, Laffy Taffy, licorice, and stuff."

Candy. Check.

"And bring marshmallows, chocolate bars, and graham crackers for making s'mores. And hot chocolate, because you'll need to fix that every morning before flag salute."

More goodies. Check.

"And help them prepare and practice a skit, including props."

Skit. Check.

"And you need to have a ward T-shirt, for unity. So get with the girls and tie-dye some or something."

T-shirts. Check.

"And you'll need something else for unity, like bandanas all in one color or headbands or something."

Craft store. Check.

"And you'll have to clean up every shred of anything on the ground before you leave or the guy who runs the place, who's like

Hitler, won't check you out on Saturday morning and you'll have to wait hours for him to come back. Not a spec of glitter, not a bottle cap, not a wrapper. You have to rake it all back to look like no one was ever there."

Hitler. Check.

"And you'll have to supervise the girls on latrine duty or kitchen duty—wherever they get assigned to clean."

Cleaning. Check.

"And you'll need to go with them on all their activities to make sure they get their certifications."

No naps. Check.

"And they have to use the buddy system. If someone wants to go off alone, you have to accompany them."

Herding cats. Check.

"And by Wednesday it's meltdown day and friendships start falling apart and the girls start crying, and some of them say they're sick and need to go home, so you have to make them stay."

Work miracles. Check.

"And they're not supposed to call their parents or their boyfriends, so you have to make sure they aren't sneaking cell phones in."

Police crowd control. Check.

"And make sure they don't bring any food in their duffle bags, not even a gum wrapper, because bears can smell it—and while *your* food will be locked in the bear box, *theirs* won't, so you have to be adamant about that."

Bear attacks. Check.

"And bring plenty of ant spray and mosquito spray."

Becoming part of the food chain. Check.

"And sunscreen."

Being an oily, stinky mess. Check.

"And you want to win awards as a camp, so you have to get them to sing the camp songs really loud every morning."

Deafening rowdiness. Check.

"And every day you need to make up a new jingle for the jingle competition."

Become a composer and lyricist. Check.

"And bring lanterns because once it's dark, you can't find your way to the outhouses."

Stumbling through the woods. Check.

"And you can take your cell phone, but it won't work. There's only one spot in the parking lot where you can get reception."

Agree to be cut off from the civilized world. Check.

I motioned for a time-out. "Couldn't we just go somewhere clean and safe and have a retreat of some sort instead of trying to join the Marines?"

She glared at me. "I hear you're a runner."

"Yes, in a well-lit neighborhood with running water, flushing toilets, plenty of fresh food, and a soft bed at night."

"Well, trust me. This experience will be the highlight of these girls' teenage years. And after a week of camp, they really develop testimonies."

Really. Then how do you explain hermits, mountain men, and campgrounds full of people still mourning the death of Jerry Garcia and playing the guitar all night? I don't see a whole lot of testimony-building there.

"Couldn't we do service projects and have firesides and a skit and meaningful moments in a beach house or something?" I asked. "I mean, I know of wards that do this in a rented lodge—or they go for three days and they find that's plenty, or—"

"I think you have everything you need," Sister Thayne said. And I was dismissed.

When Cory got home that night he took one look at me slumped over papers on the dining table and said, "I think I'll get takeout."

"Wise plan," I mumbled. I had been on the phone all afternoon trying to pin down camping equipment and permission slips.

When he got back my eyes were still crossing.

"Why didn't Sister Thayne have any of this done?" he asked.

I shook my head and dug into the hamburgers and fries. "I have no idea."

"Can't you get someone to help you?"

"Well, I called Annie and Kelly. They can come up for two days each, so that will be a lifesaver."

"Fantastic," Cory said.

The doorbell rang and I ran to open it. "Ted, you are my hero." Ted had arrived with tarps, cooking equipment, lanterns, an inflatable mattress, an ax, a shovel, a rope, a rake, and a dozen other things I hadn't thought of. We started loading them into the garage.

"I went to the same camp as a Boy Scout," he said. "And unless things have changed, you're in for it."

Suddenly I threw myself into Ted's arms. "Get me out of this, Ted," I begged. "Put on a wig and say you're my cousin and you're filling in for me."

"Yeah, that's gonna happen . . ."

"You could pull it off. I mean, if you shaved off your beard," I pleaded. "Just use a high voice and say the OllerVanKeefer women have a facial hair problem—"

If it's possible to nod sarcastically, that's what Ted was doing.

"And you *like* the outdoors!" I went on. "You *love* hiking and camping! You are made for this calling!"

Ted was nodding. "Well, good luck. Call me if you get into trouble."

I gave him a big hug and tried to keep him from pulling away. "Just think," I said. "Next time I hug you it could be from a wheelchair. I could fall off a cliff and become a paraplegic."

"I promise not to pray for that."

"Oh, very funny."

Cory hugged him too, gesturing toward all the equipment he had just brought over. "You're so great to bail her out like this."

"Well, I know Syd, and she's gonna need all the help she can get."

We waved as he drove off. "I'm in deep trouble," I muttered.

"Yep," Cory agreed.

Chapter 16

CAMP VOLDEMORT, AS I CAME to think of it—since it is The Camp That Shall Not Be Named—was even worse than described. All the pathways to each campground and activity were muddy up to your ankles and were situated along steep, rocky hillsides. The outhouses reeked. Right in the middle of it all was an ice-cold lake covered in duck droppings, in which the camp sponsored morning "polar bear swims" for the crazy people. Oh, um, I mean *the hardy people*.

Everything Sister Thayne mentioned was true—some a little truer than others. Mosquitoes were not only out and about, they were starving for fresh meat, and we were the first campers of the summer.

Right away my allergies kicked in. Normal people don't mind this so much, but I wear hard contact lenses. I know, I know, this is something only old people wear, as a rule, but it's what my eye doctor prescribed, and I had no idea I was going to be in a cyclone of pollen for an entire week. So several times a day I dropped to my knees in agony and tried to take out a contact, rinse my eye, and put the contact back in again. And while I was down there, I figured I might as well pray for rescue.

The first day we gathered in the open-air pavilion where meals were served—no cafeteria-style dining at this ultrahardy campground. I could hear the steady beat of helicopter blades approaching. "We're being rescued!" I shouted without thinking. A couple of other camp directors rolled their eyes.

As the helicopter passed overhead without landing, the raucous cheering and singing began. "Amy, Amy, strong and able—get your elbows off the table!" The girls were chanting the familiar song that forces various campers to jump up and run around the table to the cheers and laughter of the others. I know this is supposed to teach etiquette, but isn't it worse to yell at the top of your lungs? I'm just saying.

I thought about the earplugs Donna had given me, promising I would be glad I had them. They were back in my tent and nearly a mile of mud lay between me and the earplugs.

Next, it was explained that every day we'd have a different dinner table, rotating around to make it fair, since some of the tables were a little hike away from the food line. The idea was to locate your table then find the bin containing paper plates and cups at the end of the table. At this point you could come back to the food line and end up dead last behind everyone else.

"Are you kidding?" I whispered to myself. Why chase around trying to find your table then come all the way back to the pavilion entrance to get in line? Why not just spend ten bucks, get all the paper goods you need for your girls for a week, hand them out before each meal, and get right into the food line?

"You're overthinking this," Annie said, who—BLESS HER HEART FOREVER—came up to camp to help me.

"Well, I think somebody is *under*thinking it," I said. "Seriously. Why not be efficient?"

Annie laughed. "*Syd Takes on Girls' Camp*. Film at eleven."

The next day the girls earned various charms and certifications by rock climbing, zip-lining, swimming, and canoeing.

"That swimming sure looks a lot like crawling through muck," I said to Annie. "I wouldn't get in that lake if the entire forest were on fire."

"The lake would probably catch on fire too," she said. Good point.

We went to the craft area to make friendship bracelets for cancer patients. "See? Now I like this," I said, and helped some of the girls.

But, I thought to myself, *it could be done anywhere—even inside a clean building.*

Eventually it was time to attach charms to our necklaces, which looked like brass paper clips linked together but were actually fishing snap swivels. I'd seen Ted use these to go fishing, and they weren't a "snap" to operate, believe me. Have you ever pulled apart a snap swivel to attach it to another one? Unless you have fingernails of steel, it will cut right through them and leave you mangled for the week.

"Who thought of this?" I asked Marcy, the Young Women president, who (THANKFULLLY!) came to camp as well. "And then," I went on, "get this. They showed it to someone else who actually said, 'yeah—great idea!' Seriously! Is this not the most ridiculous way to make a necklace that you've ever seen in your life?"

Marcy was laughing, and finally one of the girls offered to make mine for me. I hadn't even been there twenty-four hours and already I was finding gross inefficiencies.

Next up were the destiny classes, glorious moments of religious instruction where the girls hear inspiring talks given by stake Young Women leaders. And, of course, they get a charm to attach to their necklaces.

I sat on a rock with Annie to listen to one of the speakers, but we were too far away to hear, so I just swatted away spiders.

Annie leaned over. "I would rather be getting a Pap smear than this." (Which, you've got to admit, would make a great T-shirt slogan.)

I smiled. "Okay," I whispered back. "I would rather be getting a mammogram."

"I'd rather have a colonoscopy," she said.

"Fine," I said. "I would rather be in hard labor, giving birth."

Somehow this made us feel better and we joined our group as the girls hiked back to the other side of the lake.

Every morning we rose with the birds to get the hot cocoa going and make it to the flag ceremony, scrambling through the brush to get there before points were deducted. We somehow created a new jingle every day about how much better our ward was than all the others or about the mosquitoes or the outhouses.

We also sang insane camp songs, including, "Don't gimme that tea, no tea, don't gimme that pop, no pop, just gimme that milk—moo, moo, moo, moo." And as we sang we pulled on each others' fingers to simulate cow udders. There was even a booklet of such songs—a booklet! Do the Navy SEALS do this? I think not.

The camp supervisor (Hitler, remember?) gave us a long speech about all the rules, and later I pulled him aside.

"I have a question," I said. "We're all locking our food up in a big metal box with a key," I said.

"The bear box. Yes?"

"Well, we share that box with another ward, and yet there's only one key, so we have to hang it on a tree limb after we use it. Problem is, nobody ever hangs it in the same place, and sometimes it's missing altogether, so it's hard to access our food."

He just kept listening. "So I was thinking," I said. "Since I trust them and they trust me, why do we have to lock it? I mean, truly, do we think bears have opposable thumbs and can take the padlock out? Why can't we just let it hang there and then get in and out of the box as we please?"

"Well, that's camp protocol," he said. "The leaders have to lock the box and then open it with a key."

I smiled. "May I ask why?"

"Well, you're the only group of girls we have here," he explained. "All the rest of the summer it's Boy Scout troops."

I waited to hear the problem.

"And they lock each other in the bins," he said.

"Oh, for crying out loud!" I said. "Are you joking?"

"Nope. That's why we have the protocol."

I shook my head. "Well, our girls are not going to do that," I said. Who would have even thought of that? "Could we have a different rule for when we're here?"

"Nope. Same rules," he said, and marched off.

I felt as if I'd been talking to a robot.

I also felt like a candy and water-bottle dispenser, handing out all that I could to our starving girls.

Every night we'd gather around the fire (don't even ask how hard it is to build—light, fan, and then avoid the smoke of a fire every night). But this was when I could finally get the girls to hold still long enough to read them a story and then try to have a gospel discussion. I told them to be leaders in their families. I bore my testimony. I challenged them to stay morally strong and marry in the temple one day. I told them to be each other's support system at school. It was the best time of the day, but all too short. Okay, fine, I also slipped and told them that unless they studied hard in school, this is how they'd have to live all the time.

And then it was time to climb into our sleeping bags, pray we wouldn't find any snakes or spiders in them, and try to imagine that all the snapping, croaking, whooshing sounds were just friendly forest animals, not psychopaths on the loose looking for a camp full of young women.

One morning I escorted two of our girls down to the lake for the polar bear swim. "I'm so proud of you," I said. And I meant it— not only did they get up early and go into a freezing lake, but they somehow mentally blocked the image of the duck poop, for which I felt they should get a gigantic medal, not just a little polar bear charm.

All too soon Annie had to leave. "I'm going to take a hot shower when I get home and sit down with a bowl of ice cream and watch television."

"I'm not listening," I said, hugging her. "Thanks for coming up here."

"You owe me."

"I know that."

She winked at me. "I think some of these women just want a week away from their kids. That's why you can't talk them into a shorter camp. My sister's ward in Provo only goes half this long. And I'm pretty sure they have flushing toilets."

I sighed. It was Wednesday, and sure enough, several girlfriends were mad at each other and several others were saying they felt sick and wanted to go home. A shorter camp would certainly take care of meltdown day.

Marcy was my inspiration—tireless, committed, all those things I was not. "If camping is so great," I whispered to her, "Why don't people do it all the time?"

Seriously. Who thinks it's a fun vacation to drive off and pretend you're homeless for a week?

The next day I slit my wrist. No, it's not what you're thinking. Besides, it was the back of my wrist. It caught the jagged edge of a boulder, so I went to the nurse's station.

As I expected, they were talking about all the girls who were coming in with (mostly imaginary) illnesses, trying to go home early.

"You need a polygraph in here," I said as they bandaged me up. "That should be the first stop. Make sure they're telling the truth before they waste your time." *Why am I the only person who thinks of these things?*

"A lot of girls try to go home to avoid cleanup on Saturday," one of our girls told me when I got back.

"What?"

She smiled. "You'll see."

Oh, great. A grand finale to look forward to.

That night Kelly arrived and I felt like a prisoner finally getting a visitor. I held her so long I thought she might suffocate, entirely possible given that I was wearing about four pounds of mosquito repellent and sunscreen. Kelly, a fitness trainer and the most darling woman in the entire stake, had elected to go on the crazy-hike-into-the-wilderness-for-three-days, which let me off the hook and for which she will probably be included in my will.

That night my bladder woke me at 2 AM and I fumbled for the lantern so I could get to the outhouse. We all slept in our jeans and sweatshirts to insulate against the cold, so I stepped outside the tent fully dressed. I was sharing a tent with Marcy, and since I hadn't wanted to wake her, I waited until I was outside to flick on the lantern. Nothing. I flicked the switch again. Nothing. I felt for the battery compartment and made sure it was fastened tightly. I shook the lantern. Nothing. Of all times to have a short in the wiring! It was a moonless night, and without my contacts in, a starless one as well. It was so black you couldn't even make out the shapes of trees, let alone a pathway. I knew the outhouse was straight ahead and up a hill to the left, so I tried to walk from memory.

Where was it? I was in a thicket now, and I couldn't remember a thicket like that by the outhouse. I backed out and tried again, a little farther up the hill. Still no facilities.

Finally I decided I could just pull down my pants and squat in the bushes. No one was around; the whole world was asleep. So I did. Only it's been twenty-five years since I was a little girl doing this on family vacations, and I was, to say the least, grossly out of practice. My jeans were soaking.

"No, no!" I hissed. "This cannot be happening to me." I peeled off my wet pants and headed back to camp. At least I had other pants in my suitcase. Amazingly, I found a garbage can lined with a trash bag and tossed my jeans into it.

Back at the tent I realized I had a splitting headache and fumbled for the Tylenol I was supposed to check in at the nurse's station but decided to keep with me in direct defiance of the rules. Quietly I unscrewed the cap, took out two pills, and swallowed them. Only they got stuck in my throat and wouldn't go down. I felt around for a water bottle. Empty! I found another one. Also empty!

By now I was gagging and my mouth was watering, but no matter how hard I tried to swallow, the pills were stuck. At home if this happened, I would eat something—a pinch of bread usually did the trick. But we weren't allowed to have food in our tents. And the bear box was even farther away than the outhouse.

I felt around. What could I possibly swallow to push the pills down? I found some Kleenex and tore off a wad, chewed it for a second, and then swallowed it. And then another one. Finally the pills dislodged and went at least partway down into my esophagus. I was miserable, but at least I was not going to throw up.

I put on clean clothes and got back into bed. I could feel the knot of tissue in my chest, and would have given anything for a drink of water at that point. Again, I ask you, do Navy SEALs have to wet their pants and swallow Kleenex?

Every day we tried to win an award for the most spirit in shouting our jingle, or the first ones there, or the most badges earned. And we could never quite do it.

"We've got to win the cleanest camp award," I told our girls. "It's our only hope, and we cannot go home in disgrace without winning anything." They nodded solemnly.

The next morning a few of them helped me straighten up the camp. We picked up every possible piece of trash, even microscopic cookie crumbs and fishing lures. I sat down to read scriptures at our picnic table, and one of the girls joined me. It was a weird, quiet moment—and then, as if the heavens had shined on us and a cone of yellow light was beaming down on our campsite, along came the Laurels who inspected each morning for the Clean Camp Award.

"Wow, this looks pretty good," one of them said.

"Oh, please," I said, falling to my knees and clasping my hands together. "We NEED this award. You've GOT to give us the Clean Camp Award!" Shameless? Absolutely. But after nearly a week in the wilderness I had lost all pride.

They laughed then looked in my tent. Tidy as could be. And then, in a miraculous moment, they skipped the giant blue tent in which eight of our girls were camping—and which was a disgraceful shambles—and went to the next tent, which Kelly had just set up and which was immaculate. One of them turned and gave me a thumb's up.

I gasped and turned to Amber, the girl reading scriptures with me. "I think we might get it!" I said. Her eyes lit up and we high-fived.

I saw Hitler after lunch that day, and asked him just how serious the bear problem was.

"Well, there's really only one bear," he said.

"What?" I said. "Wouldn't it be more cost-effective to tranquilize one bear and move it into the mountains where other bears congregate than to build all these bear boxes and make thousands of campers go through all this hassle to hide their food?"

He missed my point. "Well, actually he's not much trouble and rarely comes close to the camp area."

But we were still jumping through hoops and going to a lot of trouble to lock up our food—didn't that register?

"I'll tell you what they use when they want to trap a bear," he continued.

I was picturing a honeypot like Winnie the Pooh enjoyed in so many storybook tales.

"Marshmallows," he said. "They love 'em."

And then he walked off. *Excuse me?* Weren't marshmallows—for making s'mores—on top of the list of what we should bring? Weren't there hundreds of marshmallows, if not thousands, within a square mile of here? Were we nuts?

That afternoon I got to chat with one of the girls whose mom always rewarded her after girls' camp with a day at the spa, a facial, and a pedicure.

My mouth was nearly watering. "That sounds heavenly," I said. I could almost feel the warm, sudsy water around my feet.

Soon we were gathered together for an award ceremony. I had lost all track of time and space, had no idea what day it was, and had been reduced to living like an animal. The only thing that mattered was getting the Clean Camp Award.

First they presented charms and pins to girls who had fallen down slopes, had gotten rope burns while rock climbing, and who had been bruised by valiant efforts to carry canoes.

"I am so confused," I said to Marcy. "We're awarding charms for undergoing torture?"

She smiled.

"I'll bet they do this at Camp Guantanamo," I whispered. "Okay, Achmed, come on up here. Achmed survived waterboarding! Yay, Achmed! He gets a waterboarding charm!"

Now Marcy was giggling and shaking her head.

And then they announced the Clean Camp Award—and it went to us! I leapt from my bench and dashed up to the stage to accept a gold-painted toilet plunger then proudly held it aloft for photographs.

This tells you how far into the realm of mental illness I had sunk. Not only was I thrilled to receive a toilet plunger, but I was actually missing Peanut. Now that's cause for lockup.

At dinner that night I met a Young Women leader from another ward who had moved to California from Idaho about a year ago. April was single and about thirty-seven or so. Cute, spunky, strong testimony. Perfect for Ted. *So this is why I was meant to come here,* I thought to myself. I am going to set him up with this woman and she's going to be my new sister-in-law. I struck up a conversation with her and hinted that I might have someone in mind for her. "I'll call you," I said. Finally!

On the final night they honestly served funeral potatoes. I tried to ignore the symbolism, but then realized I could be dead by morning, so maybe this was the most appropriate dish for a last supper. No, wait, I remembered—I can't die until I get Ted married to a wonderful LDS girl.

I'd heard the highlight of camp was testimony time around the campfire, when the members of the bishopric came with their wives. It took several minutes for the girls to gather their courage, but most of them stood and expressed their beliefs and their gratitude for the restored gospel.

One of my favorite girls stood and tearfully let everyone know how much it meant to her to "talk about spas and facials" with Sister Syd. Oh, my. I could feel the bishop's eyes burning through my head, but I just stared at the fire and refused to look up. Hey. If the truth be known, that was one of my favorite moments too. In fact, I had really gotten to know these girls and loved every one of them by week's end.

But the warmth and joy of that evening soon came to an end, and morning brought the dreaded Pack-Up Day. Here's when all Ted's tools came in handy as we tried to restore our campsite to movie-set standards (so a troop of Boy Scouts could arrive on Monday and push all the logs and rocks away again so they could set up their tents).

We hauled trash, we packed duffle bags, we rolled up sleeping bags, we pried stakes out of the ground, we folded up our tents, and we made a virtual mountain of gear for one of our wonderful ward members to load into his pickup truck. The workers quickly distinguished themselves from the slackers, and I saw why so many girls wanted to go home early and miss this magical moment. I had to prod several of them to hurry along, since we had an early inspection time.

I noticed one of the younger gals crying as she tried to fold her tent.

"What's the matter?" I asked.

"I can't remember how my dad said I have to fold it. And he's really detailed and the tent has to be folded just so."

By now I was exhausted, and in no mood to deal with one more drop of drama, especially from a grown man, so I knelt down and helped her fold it quickly, but probably not accurately. "Look," I said, "it's a TENT. It's not origami. And if your dad isn't happy with the way it's folded, you tell him to call me." I was ready with both barrels if he so much as made a peep about it.

Hitler checked us off when he came by for inspection and we all jumped into the air and cheered, then headed to the parking lot.

"So how did you like camp?" It was one of the cheery stake leaders who does this every year—eagerly. Her necklace was loaded with dozens of charms. "Didn't you find it transformative?"

"I did," I said. What I didn't say was that I had transformed into a haggard mountain woman with bloodshot eyes, matted hair, throbbing ears, and hairy legs. Too bad it wasn't Halloween; my costume would have been perfect.

I loaded four girls into my minivan and the rest into other vehicles and we finally headed down the mountain. I dropped the loudest one off first, then dropped off the borrowed camping gear, then went home. I hugged and kissed the kids, even hugged Peanut, then ran upstairs, saw the handle to the toilet, and almost cried with joy. I peeled off my filthy clothes then stood under the shower with a loofah and a bar of soap. After I dried off, Ellie was knocking at the bathroom door.

"Mom," she called, "can we have funeral potatoes tonight?"

"Absolutely," I called back. I couldn't imagine anything more fitting.

Chapter 17

TED CAME BY THAT EVENING to pick up his tools and join us for dinner. I told him again and again how his gear truly saved me. Without that and my two good friends who came up to share my misery, I don't know how I could have survived.

Mom and Dad had helped tremendously with Juliet and the other kids while I was gone, so I asked them to stay as well.

Ted picked up my snap swivel necklace with five or six wimpy charms hanging from it. "What's this?" he said.

"Hey, I'm proud of that," I said. "I earned every one of those dinky little doodads."

He laughed. "I'll bet you did." Then he saw the golden plunger. "Trust you to win an award for keeping clean."

I shrugged; we all knew it wasn't going to be for archery.

I told the stories of my pants-wetting, my Kleenex-swallowing, and my countless bouts avoiding mosquitoes and ankle-deep mud.

"Did you go to the rifle range and learn to shoot?" Cory asked.

I gave him a look. "Are you kidding? There's a reason we have gun laws, and I'm the reason. There is certain information I shouldn't have."

He laughed. "Undoubtedly."

I was eager to hear every detail of the week while I'd been away, and was glad Mom stepped in as the tooth fairy for me when Hayden lost a tooth. Ellie played her latest piano piece, Joshua read me a new beginner book, and I felt as if I'd been gone a month.

The kids had arranged for a sundae bar for dessert, and I piled on every topping. Ice cream never tasted so good.

We played games for an hour or so, and then it was the kids' bedtime. Mom and Dad headed out, and I asked Ted if he could wait a few minutes. I walked with him out to his truck.

"I met a really neat single sister at camp," I said.

"Oh no," Ted said and started getting into his truck. "I am not computer dating with you as my computer."

"She'd be perfect for you," I pleaded. "She's really cute and smart—"

"I hope you didn't make her any promises."

"No, no," I assured him. "I just got her number, that's all. And you've got to call her."

"What makes you think I'm even looking to get married? Most marriages I see are pretty unhappy ones."

"Sheesh, Ted." I laughed. "Of course they are. If a happy marriage didn't take work, everyone would have one."

Ted sighed. "So how come she's not married yet if she's so terrific?"

"Hey," I said, gesturing with both hands up, pointing at Ted.

"No, this sort of thing never works. Besides, I'm not even active. I'm sure she's looking for an entirely different guy."

"Maybe she's your soul mate. Maybe you'll both take one look at each other, and—"

"Syd, I have beer in my refrigerator."

"So take it out."

Now he looked up at me, lowering his eyebrows. "This is just another of your crazy attempts to get me back to church."

"Would that be so terrible? Please? Just tell me you'll call her. Just ask her to meet you for a soda someplace. And then if you don't click, fine. But at least call her." I tucked the number into his shirt pocket.

He rolled his eyes and backed out of the driveway.

"You promised!" I shouted after him.

"Did not," he shouted back.

Cory came out as I was waving good-bye. "What was all that about?"

I told him how I'd met the ideal woman for Ted to marry.

"I'm sure he was thrilled to hear that," Cory said.

"Okay," I admitted, "he wasn't thrilled. I know he sees me as this interfering, meddling little sister."

"Which, of course, you're not."

I smiled and looped my arm through Cory's. "I have only his best interests at heart. Besides, don't you want him to be happy like us?"

Cory kissed me on the forehead. "Actually, I do."

"I told him good marriages take work."

"Hard, excruciating work," Cory teased.

"But you're worth it," I teased back, and kissed him. "And anyway, it's nowhere near as hard as girls' camp."

A week went by, then two, and I couldn't stand it any longer. I called Ted to see if he had called April yet. Cory and I were both in the bathroom getting ready for the day. I was bouncing Juliet on one hip.

Ted picked up on the second ring. "Uh, I thought this note said to wait until April to call her," he said. "Says right here, 'April.'"

"Very funny."

"Yeah, I actually called her one night," Ted said.

"Seriously?"

"Nope. Just thought I'd yank your chain."

"Ted! Stop teasing me. Could I have you both over for dinner and maybe you could meet her that way?"

"Oh, for crying out loud, Syd. I don't want to do this."

"But I'm begging!"

"Look, if I call her one time will you leave me alone about it? Don't ambush me, don't set me up on a blind date, just let me call."

"Okay," I agreed. "That's totally fair."

Ted laughed. "No, it's not fair. It's Syd getting her way again. What's fair about it?"

"Okay, fair or not, I accept your offer to call her. And now I have your word."

"Fine."

A few seconds went by.

"So when are you going to call her?" I asked.

"Good-bye, Syd."

"Let me know how it goes," I pleaded.

"Good-bye." Ted hung up.

"Well," I said, turning to Cory, "he agreed to call her."

Cory laughed. "To get you off his back."

"Hey, I don't care what his reason is, at least he's doing it."

Cory shook his head. "We need to rent you out to prisons and rehab facilities."

"I don't find that amusing."

Cory tied his necktie. "But it would work."

The next day Ted called. He had spoken to her, said she seemed very nice, and he was meeting her for lunch.

"Lunch!" I gasped. "That's fabulous!"

"It's just a little bakery place that serves salad," Ted said. "Just a quick thing."

I called Cory at work. "Do you think I could get hired there really fast so I could peek out of the kitchen at them?" I asked.

"Stop being Lucy," he said. "Just let it happen. And don't get your hopes up."

Too late. Their date was on Saturday, since April worked as a guidance counselor at the local college on weekdays.

All Saturday afternoon I paced, waiting for the phone to ring with Ted's report. What if she thought he needed too much rescuing? What if he thought she was too quiet? Or too chatty? By evening I couldn't stand it and had to call.

"I wondered how long you could stand the suspense," Ted said.

"So you were deliberately not calling," I said.

"Correct."

"Well, now you know the limits of my patience. So how did it go?"

"Terrible."

"Are you joking or being serious?"

"I'm serious," he said. "For one thing, I ordered coffee."

"Oh, Ted," I moaned. "Why would you do that?"

"I just did it out of habit."

I sighed a loud, exasperated sigh. "So then what happened?"

"So then she said she thought I was LDS."

"Of course."

"And I said that yes, I was, but I'm not active. Did you know she has the annoying habit of drumming her fingers on the table?"

"Hey. I would have the annoying habit of slapping you silly," I snapped.

Ted was drinking something and I didn't even want to ask what. "So then," he said, taking another swallow, "she asked me why I wasn't active."

"Well, at least she didn't storm out of there," I said.

"Oh, that's coming," Ted said. "So I said I wasn't sure, but I probably had an authority problem. Hey, at least I can admit it."

"So is this when she walked out?"

"Oh no. It escalated. She asked me how long I plan to resist authority and cut off my chances for happiness. To be honest, she sounded a lot like you."

"Hmm." I wasn't sure if this was a good thing or a bad thing.

"So then I told her I don't have a timetable, and that I'd like to ask her a few questions myself." He took another sip. "And that's when she stood up, nearly knocking the table over, leaned over, and said, 'I counsel confused teenagers every day. I don't need another one on the weekends.'"

"And that's when she took off," I said.

"Yep."

I sighed and a few seconds passed. "So was the salad any good?"

"Fair."

"Ted, I'm so sorry."

"I know you are," he said. "I knew this thing would blow up and then you'd feel terrible. But I know you meant well. You just need to back off and stop trying to control everything. That was Mom's problem, you know."

I closed my eyes and tried not to imagine which of my kids would feel like Ted—overdirected, overmanaged. "She loves you so much," I said. "We talked about you a couple of months ago and she would give anything to go back in time and let you feel more acceptance."

"She said that?"

"Yes. She really regrets how she did things. How she demanded so much."

"Hmm."

"Parenting is hard, Ted. You have to parent a different way for each child. And invariably your natural style will work with some and be the exact opposite of what another one needs."

"Sounds pretty complicated."

"Well," I admitted, "it's definitely not how it's advertised. But Ted, it is so worth it. It's the most exciting, rewarding thing I've ever done."

"And you don't get an A or a medal for it," he said.

"No. In fact, you get thrown up on, disobeyed, and resented."

Ted laughed. "Uh, are those the selling points?"

"But it's worth it, Ted. Accolades don't matter."

"Whoa. Never thought I'd hear an OllerVanKeefer say that."

"But it's true. And Mom now realizes that more than anyone."

"Well," he said. "That's good to know, I guess."

We both paused for a minute. Then I told him again how sorry I was that his meeting with April went so wrong.

"You know," Ted said, "if you'd let people live their own lives, you wouldn't have to apologize so much."

"Wise and true," I said. "See you Monday."

Ellie had been sitting at the breakfast bar, leaning on one elbow to prop herself up. "So his date didn't work out?

"No," I said. And I had been so sure it would. "I guess I need to pray about things and listen for inspiration before I go jumping headlong into what I think is a good idea."

Ellie chewed this over then said, "I have that sometimes," as if being impulsive was a disease.

"You do?"

"Oh, boy. Like that time I tried to be friends with that new girl, Tacie. Remember that?"

"I do." Tacie turned out to be a conniving, manipulative brat whose sole mission was to climb over everyone else on her way to the top.

"She ended up cheating off my paper, stealing my lunch, even saying my blue jacket was hers. She spent half her time in the principal's office."

I remember last year having been torn between telling Ellie to try to help the girl and telling her to get as far away from Tacie as possible. We had even invited Tacie over—once—before we realized she had theft issues. That episode ended with Ellie crying and Tacie having to be driven home two hours early. As I expected, a careless, rude mother answered the door dressed in a tight tank top and a thong. I kid you not.

What is it about moms whose top priority is to be "hot"? Every time I see one—at the airport, at a restaurant, anywhere (except at a library)—their kids are acting up and out of control. Somebody should write a thesis on this. I've also noticed there's often a grandma in tow, and she's the only one actually trying to maintain some semblance of acceptable behavior among her grandkids. But the mom is tuned out, teetering on her high heels and ignoring the children entirely.

I'm also a little worried about the kids of those young moms who exercise like demons until they're a size two then sign up for every plastic surgery they can. Like the "hot mom," their priorities are mixed up. They're insecure, self-obsessed, and raising kids who'll be just like them.

Fortunately for us, Tacie moved a few months later. But some-where, she's terrorizing a new classroom of kids and headed for a life of misery. And, as Cory pointed out, you can't save everyone. You can be kind, you can offer to help in any way possible, you can try to share the gospel with them, but the bottom line is that these people need therapists. And most of them don't see that, so they never get the help they really need.

And their numbers are growing.

Chapter 18

By NOVEMBER I LEARNED I WAS EXPECTING AGAIN, so I bowed out of the annual harvest brunch I usually served for the neighbors. Morning sickness made it all but impossible to cook, so I lay on the sofa with a box of saltine crackers and a heaping of guilt.

"Hey, let one of them step up and throw the brunch," Cory said.

"It's a fellowshipping thing," I moaned.

Cory sat beside me and smoothed my hair. "You push yourself too hard. You need to—" he stopped.

"You were going to say *relax,* weren't you?"

He smiled. "I've learned that certain words set you off," he said. "And that one's at the top of the list."

I laughed. "But you're right," I said. "I need to realize the world won't end if we miss one brunch."

"There you go."

"But I hope I'm better by Thanksgiving," I said. "We're supposed to host it this year."

"Be thankful you have such capable siblings who can step in and do it," Cory said.

This was true. That's not all: Chad and Neal always travel here with their families, so there would be no shortage of helpful cooks on hand.

Then, as if right on cue, five days before Thanksgiving I got up and felt as if I were alive again. The first trimester had passed, along with all the queasiness. And just as I was feeling alive, I got a call about a death.

Our former stake president had suffered a cardiac arrest that morning and had died within minutes. I couldn't believe it. Yes, he was in his eighties, but he had seemed so vigorous and healthy at our last stake conference. President Petersen had been instrumental in the building of the Sacramento California Temple, and the shock wave rippled through the whole region.

Our kids couldn't remember him, but Neal and Chad had both left on their missions while he was in office and had great love for him. It felt like losing a dear uncle. Even Ted remembered several meetings with him and had said he would never forget the love and tenderness of that man.

We each wrote letters to Sister Petersen, sharing our memories of her wonderful husband, and sent them off in a manila envelope. Cory and I joined some other ward members in ordering a funeral spray of gladiolas, mums, and orange roses—his favorite.

It seemed surreal, as it always does when you lose someone who's been a fixture in your life. The day before Thanksgiving, we joined throngs of mourners packing the pews and cultural hall. Chairs had even been arranged in the auxiliary rooms to accommodate the huge crowd. Chad and Neal were sad about President Petersen's death but grateful they could be in town for his funeral.

Donna was bustling at the back of the cultural hall, arranging scrapbooks on various tables and photo boards on easels. Ted, who had come with us, whispered to me, "This doesn't have to be an exhibit at the world's fair."

"You know Donna," I winked. "Nothing can be done halfway." And, honestly, this was a fitting tribute for such a remarkable man. I knew his family would appreciate her hard work.

A meal for just the close family was planned for that afternoon at the current stake president's home.

"Do you think they'll have funeral potatoes?" Ellie whispered to me.

Ted heard her and smiled. "Of course they will," he said.

The service was incredible. Maybe it was because President Petersen was incredible. While one or two funny stories were shared, more was said about the kindness he'd shown to others. The sacrifices he'd made. The charity he'd given to so many. How Christlike he'd been. I felt I was hearing stories about a scripture hero, only I had known this one in my own lifetime.

President Petersen had a way of seeing everyone from the angle of a loving parent. It was God's perspective, really. He loved everyone and ached when they tripped up, but it never diminished his love. No one could offend him; no one could make him less than generous and forgiving.

It reminded me of a talk President Petersen had given once. He said that every person you will ever meet has a patriarchal blessing waiting for him or her. And from that minute on, I thought about that. I'd see rowdy guys stumbling out of a bar and I'd think, "If they could join the Church and a patriarch could lay his hands upon their heads, God would have a message for those guys." I'd see football stadiums filled with people and I'd think the same thing. I'd think it when I saw crowds bustling through Grand Central Station in New York. Criminals in handcuffs on TV. There is a blessing waiting for every single person. Amazing. It made me a better missionary too. It was a constant reminder that God knew and loved this person, whoever it was at the moment, and that I needed to do the same.

"Wow," Cory said, wiping his eyes after the service. I looked around. Men and women alike were dabbing at their eyes and probably vowing to be more like President Petersen. I think we all were.

That afternoon I put on an apron and began making pies and stuffing for the following day. The kids were at Mom and Dad's playing with their cousins since the large farmhouse was always where Neal and Chad stayed with their families when they came to town. I assumed Donna was in her kitchen, snapping beans and peeling yams. "And so life goes on," I said to Cory.

He was setting up the extra tables we'd need and had just brought in the tablecloths. "Yep. It's sure gonna be a sad Thanksgiving for the Petersens."

I nodded. Losing someone so close to a holiday was especially hard. And while they were blessed to know that he hadn't suffered for months on end, his death had come as a shock, something for which no one was prepared.

The phone rang. I figured it was one of the kids with another riddle (something they'd been calling with every twenty minutes or so).

But it was Jerry, Donna's husband. "Syd," he said.

I knew immediately something was wrong.

"Donna's on the way to the hospital," Jerry said, his voice shaking. "Could you and Cory meet us there?"

I assured him we were on our way, left the pie dough on the counter, and we jumped in the car.

The entire ride was a blur. Both of us were frantic, unable to imagine what could possibly have happened. Was it a recurrence of her pneumonia? We hadn't called the others yet, not wanting to alarm them and waiting to see what Jerry wanted us to do. We swept into the emergency entrance, into the cold, gray waiting room filled with urgent cases. Frightened faces like ours were looking around for help, just as we were. The intercom blared with the paging of various doctors.

We dashed up to an information window. Donna was in the emergency room, and the hospital would only allow two people in to see her. Jerry came out soon, then he and Cory went in and gave Donna a blessing.

Jerry stayed at her side while Cory came out and told me what he knew. Evidently Donna had collapsed in her kitchen, sobbing hysterically and saying she wanted to die.

"What?!" I was thoroughly astounded. "That's impossible!" Donna was the rock, the leader, the sunniest woman you ever met!

Cory shook his head. "Jerry's worried about the kids. They saw the whole thing." The top of Cory's collar was dampening with perspiration.

"What?!" I still couldn't think of another thing to say.

"I don't know," Cory went on. "It's like a nervous collapse or something. They're sedating her; after that, I guess she'll get assigned to a room."

I tried to absorb what I was hearing. "The kids. So what's happening with the kids?"

"Jerry called Mom and Dad to come and get them. So the rest of the family does know."

"How did this happen?" I asked. Of course, I knew Cory couldn't answer; I was just thinking aloud.

Cory just shook his head. "Poor Donna."

I asked the nurse if I could see her and went in at once. Jerry was leaning over her, trying to soothe her, and Donna was crying.

"Honey," I said, standing on the other side of the bed and taking her hand. "I'm here."

She looked over at me. "You're wearing an apron," she slurred, almost through a fog.

I looked down and realized I had torn out of the house so fast I hadn't even thought about what I was wearing.

I smiled and hugged her. "You're gonna be okay," I whispered. "We love you so much."

Jerry squeezed my other hand. Donna drifted off to sleep from whatever was in her IV, and we stepped away to talk. "I don't know what brought this on," Jerry said. "She was just fixing food for tomorrow, and suddenly I heard this screaming and crying." He paused, hesitant to say what came out next. "She's had a mental breakdown, Syd. She was talking nonsense—" Jerry burst into tears.

I held him and let him cry. "She'll pull through this, Jerry. You know how strong she is."

Jerry took a deep breath and tried to compose himself. "We have her on some medication to help her sleep."

"Anything you need, we'll do," I said.

"I know," he said. "I know. I just wonder if—" he stopped.

"If what?"

"I've seen this in patients before," he said. "Sometimes they recover, and sometimes—" He paused. "Well, they just don't function very well afterward."

"But Donna's such a trooper," I said. "I mean, who has more determination than Donna? And you guys gave her a blessing—"

Jerry nodded. "I'm going to stay right here with her," he said. "I'll call you when she wakes up."

I felt numb as I walked out to Cory and then got back in the car. We speculated both silently and to each other how this could happen.

"Donna's not the nervous breakdown type," I argued as if the universe could hear me and set this right. "I mean, seriously, have you ever met anyone more capable?"

Cory shook his head. "Maybe it's something else. They'll run tests, and who knows—maybe do an MRI on her brain? Something else had to have caused this." Neither of us said it, but both of us were thinking it: *Brain tumor.*

We drove to my parents' house to collect the kids and talk about what to do. Of course, there was nothing any of us could do other than wait. We assured the children that Aunt Donna was going to recover and that everything would be fine. But having witnessed it, her children looked especially shaken. Like clockwork, we each took one of her kids and held them in our arms.

"I know it's Thanksgiving tomorrow," Dad said, "but shouldn't we have a family fast?"

"Absolutely," I chimed in. And everyone agreed. What's a turkey and dressing compared to a family emergency?

"Everything will keep," Mom said.

"In fact," Cory added, "this is probably the best way to spend Thanksgiving. Loving each other, counting our blessings, and drawing close to the Lord."

Some of the kids looked crestfallen, having looked forward to the feast for months. "We'll have a delayed Thanksgiving when Aunt Donna comes home. Then we'll celebrate with all the trimmings," I said.

And everyone focused on the hopeful future, that this crisis would pass quickly and we would return to normal living.

"Has anyone called Ted?" Mom asked, looking right at me.

"Oh, my gosh," I said. "I'll call him right now." I stepped away to use my cell phone in a quieter room.

Suddenly I was struck by a flood of anger. It caught me so off guard that I had to sit down quickly.

Why was I feeling angry? What was all this about? I literally felt paralyzed for a moment, unable to dial the phone. Was this just pregnancy hormones?

And then I realized I was angry with Donna! How could she do anything other than show Ted that the gospel solves everything? The gospel is the key to happiness! How could Donna set such a terrible example for Ted? How would we ever get him back into the Church if it looked as if an active member could still have a nervous breakdown?

I knew it was absolutely crazy. Tears of shame filled my eyes. It was as if I had an angel and a devil on opposite shoulders, arguing.

How could I be angry at my poor sister, who was in the hospital this very minute?

Yet how could she do this after all my years of working so hard to get Ted back to church? How could she do this to *me?*

Yet how could I not realize that all people—even Church members—are human and need support, understanding, and empathy?

Yet how could she be so selfish, thinking only of her own problems instead of the overarching goal of reactivating Ted?

Yet now was the time to rally as a family instead of worrying about appearances.

Realizing I was alone, I allowed myself to cry openly, sobbing loudly as I fought with my own feelings. I wanted so desperately to paint the picture for Ted that life is perfect when you're active. And here was indisputable evidence, as Cory would say, that it's not.

Both of my contact lenses had slid off center, so I had to hold the phone an inch from my eyes to see the keypad. When I gave Ted the news, he asked me if Donna was going to make it.

"Oh, I think she's definitely going to make it," I said.

"The way you're crying, I would have thought she was dying," he said.

No. Only my hopes are dying. I tried to sound a bit calmer. "No, she'll definitely pull through. It's just . . . just scary. And the kids were there when she lost it, so they're pretty upset."

"I'll be right there."

I came out of the room and looked for Cory. He could see I'd been crying and said, "You okay?"

I nodded. "Yep. Ted's coming over."

Cory kept his arm around my shoulders, and I led him off to the same quiet room where I had called Ted. At that moment I realized what a blessing it is to have an eternal companion you can allow to see your heart stripped down to the honest truth, ugly or not, and still know he'll be there for you regardless. I bared my soul. "I'm so worried that this will prove to Ted that the gospel doesn't make everything perfect."

Cory cupped my face in his hands. "Is that what you think? That Ted's been waiting for proof that the gospel will solve everything?" He pulled me to the guest bed and we sat down. "Syd, the gospel is the best road to happiness on this earth. But we'll still have challenges. We'll still have sorrows. And Ted knows that."

"But I want him to see how the gospel helps us deal with our problems."

"And that means no one has their agency anymore?" he asked. "Just because we have the gospel plan doesn't mean everybody lives it."

"Are you saying Donna wasn't living it?"

Cory held my shoulders as if bracing me for an announcement. "Syd, you do realize that Donna is compulsively competitive."

"So?"

"So she has always had to be the best, the ultimate—it's not healthy. She took this perfection thing to a very sick level, Syd. She drives herself way too hard. And the gospel does not teach people to push themselves so hard that they finally collapse."

"Do you think that's what happened?"

Cory nodded. "In your heart, don't you?"

I cried and fell against his chest. "Yes. I know it. She's always been the golden girl." I grabbed a tissue and blew my nose. "She was first place in everything, champion of everything—the whole world admired her."

"That's a lot of pressure to live up to, day in and day out," Cory said. "It's extreme. It's not moderation. It's a poison."

He was right. Perfectionism poison had landed my sister in the hospital.

Chapter 19

FOR TWO DAYS DONNA DIDN'T want any visitors except Jerry and their children. I popped into their home with meals and took the kids to a matinee, since everyone was still out of school for Thanksgiving break. We had to caravan in three cars to get everybody's kids to the theater, but it was a needed diversion.

Samantha, Donna's oldest, was fifteen and was torn between crying on my shoulder and acting as if nothing had happened. Finally, on the second night, I asked her to go for a walk with me.

"Do you really want to know how I feel?" she asked after a while. "I'm embarrassed. My mom flipped out. What will everyone say when I go back to school?"

I slung an arm over her shoulders. "That really sucks," I said.

She smiled. "You're trying to talk like a teenager, Aunt Syd."

"Is it working?"

"No."

"Okay. But I do know how you feel."

Samantha rolled her eyes.

"I do!" I said. "Shall I tell you one of my feelings? I was angry because I thought it would wreck all my efforts to get your Uncle Ted reactivated."

She smiled; so I wasn't the only selfish person in the family. I pulled her to a bench where we could sit and talk.

"Look," I said. "You come from a long line of people who are all caught up in appearances. We're all frantic about what the neighbors will think, and to be honest, it's ridiculous. Grandma raised us to constantly be looking over our shoulders and making sure we were admired."

Samantha smiled. "That sounds familiar."

"Well," I went on, "the idea of pursuing excellence is good. And so is having a good reputation. But you can't be completely focused on the approval of others, Samantha. It's a dead end. And I know you're going to say this sounds corny, but the honest truth is that the only person we have to please is God."

"But isn't He the hardest one of all to please?"

"No—He's the easiest. Because all we need is a sincere, good heart. We just have to want to do the right thing and love our fellow man. Seriously, it's not that complicated. He loves us no matter what, but He's thrilled when we do the right thing. And maybe the crowds won't see it and we'll lose friends along the way, but . . ." I tried to put it simply. "If we know God is happy with us, that's where true confidence comes from. And then we won't care so much what others think."

"So what about competing? Isn't competition good?"

"I used to think it was," I said. "I was always a competitive learner—I got As to show up the other kids. But think about that: How vicious is it to want to beat someone else all the time? It's nuts."

"Our seminary teacher said the Church had them stop having competitions where you pit one side of the class against the other, because it drives the Spirit away."

"And does it?"

Samantha nodded. "I think it does. I mean, it felt that way."

"Well, there you go. And when you grow up and marry, it doesn't have to be a competition for you to have the biggest house, or the finest decorating, or the best car, or the most children, or the most gifted children—" I paused. "Let me tell you something. Wanting others to be jealous of you is based in hatred."

"Wow, Aunt Syd. That's pretty strong."

"But it's true. Think about it. Do you have love for others when you're trying to outdo them? It's one of Satan's ploys to get us to dislike each other."

Samantha thought for a moment. "I think you're right."

"Every time you want to show someone up or be better than she is, then you lose that Christlike charity we're supposed to have."

"Or when you're jealous that someone else got a better grade, or was chosen for cheerleader and you weren't—"

"Exactly!" I said. "Those horrible feelings are exactly what Satan wants us to have. And he mocks the approval of God with the approval of man. He makes us think certificates and trophies are the ultimate goal."

"You have a lot of running trophies, Aunt Syd. I saw them in your garage one time."

I laughed. "And that's where they belong. Samantha, I'm not saying it's wrong to excel or to win a trophy. I'm just saying we can't make that more important than anything else in our lives. It's like money isn't bad, but *worshipping* money is bad. Honey, I want you to do your best in school, in sports, in whatever you do. But only if you put God first."

Samantha nodded. "So my mom got sidetracked."

I hugged her. "Oh, Sammy, I know she loves Heavenly Father and has a strong testimony. I'm not saying your mom is a bad person. But, yes, she got sidetracked." I pulled back and held her shoulders. "Our whole family has gotten sidetracked, Samantha."

"Except Uncle Ted."

I thought about that. "Nope. Even Uncle Ted is sidetracked. He's sidetracked trying to prove he's not being, I don't know, controlled or something."

"I wish he'd come back to church," Samantha said. "The only time you see him there is when there's a funeral."

"I know," I said. "Not that I'm glad when someone dies, but . . ."

She laughed. "Mom says you keep his name on the prayer roll at the temple."

I nodded. "If people had any idea how much power there is in the temple, and in the prayers there, they'd beat a path to its door."

I think Samantha sensed another minilecture coming on, so she stood up. "I'm glad we went on this walk," she said.

It was quiet for a while, then she said, "So what do I say on Monday when kids ask if my mom had a nervous breakdown?"

I thought for a moment. "Just say we're not sure exactly what happened, but we're sure praying for her."

Samantha smiled. "Then how can they argue with that?"

"Exactly."

"And then it tells them I still love my mom and this isn't something to joke about."

"Exactly."

Samantha picked up her step.

"Oh, one more thing," I said as we got back to the house. "The kids who sincerely care and want to help?"

"Yeah?"

"Remember them."

She smiled and we went inside.

Ted had stopped by while we were out walking and I could hear his voice in the family room. I went in; he was talking with Daniel, Donna's thirteen-year-old.

Make that shouting. As I entered I heard Daniel shout, "Because she's a hypocrite, that's why! She tells me I have to get my Eagle by the time I'm fourteen, and be in the band, and be on the basketball team, and get straight As—and then she pulls this!"

Ted was glowering. "She did not 'pull' something. And if you can't appreciate having one of the best moms in the entire country and go visit her in the hospital, then you're just a dope, that's what."

"Uh . . ." I said, completely uncomfortable with what I was hearing on both sides but at a loss about what to say.

"Forget it!" Daniel yelled, storming out. As he got to the front door he sneered. "I'll be with my friends."

I looked back at Ted. "Wow. What happened?"

"Oh, I caught him with those idiot skateboarders in the Target parking lot," he said.

"Not all skateboarders are idiots," I said.

"No, but I know 'em when I see 'em," Ted argued. "One of them was smoking who knows what and the others looked like hoodlums. So I told Daniel to get in the truck and I brought him home. He ought to be visiting his mom with the other kids, not being ashamed of her."

I sighed. "I agree. But . . . dope?"

"Oh, I don't know if it was a cigarette or dope—"

"No." I laughed. "I mean you called Daniel a dope."

"I did?" Ted had no idea he'd said that. "Well, he is a dope."

"Okay, maybe he's doing all the wrong things right now, but . . ."

Ted patted my back. "You're right, Syd. When you're right, you're right. I shouldn't have called him that. But it just gets my goat to see him being so defiant. It's like he's doing the opposite of what Donna wants him to, just because he's a hard-headed little squirt who thinks he knows everything."

I nodded. And, you will be so proud of me, I did *not* say one word about how very much Daniel is like his Uncle Ted. Not a peep.

"Well, I really can't stay," Ted said. "I just came by to check on everyone. Looks like I've done enough damage here anyway."

I hugged him good-bye. "We might get to visit her tomorrow."

Jerry hadn't come home from making rounds at the hospital yet and had done a couple of deliveries during the night. I knew he'd be exhausted, so I invited the kids to a sleepover at their Aunt Syd's.

"With peanut-butter cream pie?" Brit asked. Brit was eleven, and already a budding foodie.

I laughed. "Yes, I'll make you peanut-butter cream pie," I said. I was already planning to drive by the parking lot to pick up Daniel. "Where's Ben?"

Nine-year-old Ben was in his room, staring at his two goldfish as they circled in their bowl. I went over and sat beside him on the edge of his bed.

"Hey, what's up?"

"It's my fault, Aunt Syd."

"What?"

His voice cracked. "I'm the one who made my mom get sick and have to go to the hospital."

"What? Who told you that?"

Ben shrugged and sniffled. "I just know."

I put my arm around him. "And how do you know?"

"Because I was the one she was talking to when it happened."

I ruffled his hair. "You did not cause it, Ben. It would have happened no matter who she was talking to, sweetie."

Ben just sniffed and kept staring at the fish.

"Hey, Ben," I said. "Do you think your goldfish wonder what kind of weird creatures we are, with such big heads and no fins?"

He thought for a moment, then smiled.

"What were you and your mom talking about when—you know, when it happened?"

"You."

"Me?"

Ben nodded. "I asked her if you knew if you were having a boy or a girl."

"That's it?"

Again, he nodded.

"Ben, that is such an innocent, normal question. Trust me, that could never upset a fly. Your mom was upset about a whole bunch of other things. It wasn't you at all, Ben."

He looked over at me. "You don't think so?"

"I know so. It would be impossible for that question to cause anything. A fly wouldn't even collapse over that."

"You talk about flies a lot, Aunt Syd."

I sighed. "Yes, apparently so. Come on. I want you guys to sleep over at my house tonight. Deal?"

Ben slid off the bed. "Deal." He grabbed some pajamas and a duffle bag then looked up. "Will you stop talking about flies?"

"Oh, absolutely," I said.

That night, Mom and Dad came by as I was slicing the two pies. "Perfect timing," I teased. "Somebody tipped you off that we were having pie."

Dad laughed. "Just a lucky break."

The kids took their slices to the family room to enjoy while watching a movie.

"You let them eat in there?" Mom asked.

"I do tonight. They need to relax."

She shrugged. "It's so terrible, isn't it? Donna is the last person I would have expected to . . . well, you know."

Good grief; she couldn't even say it. "Well," I said, "I think the pressure's been building for a long time."

Mom just shook her head in sympathy. Samantha and Brit came back in for extra napkins, and I did not want to know why.

"Hey, we have a new calling," Dad said. "We're the Young Single Adult reps."

"Oh, that's cool," Samantha said. "So what do you do?"

"Well, we contact all the young singles in our ward, let them know about upcoming activities, and try to get the less active ones out to church again."

"People like Uncle Ted?"

"Well, yes," Mom said, "except Ted would be in the regular singles group."

Dad winked. "I know what you're thinking," he said, wagging his fork like a finger. "You're wondering why they gave such an old couple this calling."

"No, I wasn't," Samantha said.

"Well," Dad went on, "to tell you the truth, I think someone younger might have better luck. I think they'd listen more to someone their own age who tells them to get off their duff and come back to church."

"What's a duff?" Samantha asked.

Dad swept his hands out from his sides. "And I rest my case."

"I guess the first thing to remember is not to use the word *duff*." I laughed.

"Or say that something sucks," Samantha added, glancing at me. Mom bristled.

"Oh, it's just something I said earlier," I said.

Now Mom *really* bristled.

"I was trying to sound young and hip," I said.

"And it didn't work," Samantha assured her.

I turned to my parents. "You guys will be great at this. A lot of kids need someone to lean on. That can't always be a peer. They need some parent-types to nurture them. A peer can't do that."

"How about grandparent-types?" Dad asked.

"Even better," I said. "You'll see. I heard a talk once about how if you assume everyone you meet is facing a terrible problem, you'll be right more than half the time. And with young single adults, I'll bet the statistics are more like 80 percent." (I was glad Cory wasn't home to catch me making up a statistic.)

"No doubt," Dad agreed.

"So just find out what their most pressing problem is and help them with it."

"If they'll confide in us," Mom said.

"Well, you build that trust," I said. "In fact, we really should treat everyone we meet that way. We should go through life with a *How can I best help you?* attitude."

Dad looked at Mom. "We raised a pretty smart cookie, wouldn't you say?"

Brit had just dashed in for another fork. "And don't say *smart cookie*," she added.

Chapter 20

THE NEXT DAY WAS SATURDAY, and as I dropped Donna's children off to Jerry, he said I could probably visit her now. Cory was with our own kids, so I dashed right to the hospital.

"Hey, you," I said as I came around the curtain.

Donna smiled but looked as weak as I've ever seen her. "Thanks for helping so much with the kids," she said.

I waved it away. "Of course! You'd do the same for me." And I stopped short of saying, *Only better. And with scrapbooks.*

"I guess I've really embarrassed the whole family."

I asked if I could sit on the bed beside her. "Are you kidding? We love you, Donna. You are not an embarrassment. We just want you to get well and come home."

"Me too," she said. "This was really a wake-up call, I guess."

I nodded, listening.

"The doctors all say I need to slow down and de . . . dele . . . deg—"

"Are you trying to say *delegate*?" I asked.

She smiled and nodded.

I laughed and squeezed her hand. "Well, I guess the first step is being able to say the word!"

She laughed too. "It's not my strongest trait."

"Well, it'll have to be," I said. "You've been Superwoman long enough."

Donna sighed. "I've had a lot of time to think," she said. "And I have a really great counselor—a psychologist—who's been working with me."

This was wonderful, in itself, that Donna could admit she needed outside help instead of trying to do it all herself.

"She's taught me so much, Syd. Everybody should have a counselor."

I laughed. "You're probably right. We all run to the doctor for physical problems, but nobody gets a shrink for emotional problems, which are ten times more common."

She smiled. "There you go again, making up statistics."

I laughed. "That's how you know it's me instead of a Swedish supermodel."

Now we both laughed and then Donna started crying.

"What?" I said, patting her and trying to offer comfort.

"See?" she said. "I can't be funny like you are. I've always been so jealous of you, Syd."

My jaw dropped. "What? Why on earth would you be jealous of *me*?"

Donna's eyes rolled as if I had asked an obvious question.

"Because you could do things I couldn't," she said. "There was your running, and that crazy peanut-butter pie—"

"Are you kidding?" I said. "I ran because it was the only thing left that you older kids hadn't already mastered! And that ridiculous pie is the easiest thing in the world to make—"

"Maybe it is," Donna said, "but mine never comes out as good as yours."

I sighed. "Are you serious? You're jealous of a pie?"

"Of the perfect Aunt Syd who makes the pie," she corrected. "And your humor, and your callings, and your statistics—"

I held up my hands in a time-out gesture. "My statistics? I make those up!"

"That's just it. I can't think on my feet and make things up like you do."

I looked around to make sure we were alone then leaned in to whisper. "Donna, my kids think I'm a big liar."

Now she laughed, tears coming easily. "You outdo me all the time."

I cracked my neck. "How about this?" I said. "You always hate it when people crack their knuckles."

"That's obnoxious," she said. "I don't envy that."

I poured her a glass of water from the pitcher on her bedside stand. "And what's this about my callings?" I said. "You don't think the Lord picks those?"

"I know," she said, taking a sip. "I've just been so competitive all my life that I can't let go, even when it's ridiculous."

I smiled at her and shook my head. At least she was examining this extreme behavior.

"I was so jealous of how thin you are, Syd."

"Are you kidding? I was always the scrawny one and you're the voluptuous one!"

Donna rolled her eyes. "Those are implants."

"What?"

Now she just stared at me. "You have no idea all the plastic surgery I've had, do you?"

"*What?*" I sounded like a broken record, but I was thunderstruck at this confession.

"I've been nearly addicted to it," she said. "I kept thinking, 'Just one more thing,' and I'd get Botox or liposuction. I've never even had pneumonia, Syd. The last time I was getting a tummy tuck."

"What?" I wanted to say, *What on earth is the matter with you?* but didn't want to start a fight.

"It's been so awful," she said, crying into a Kleenex. "And a lot of it has had to be redone. Jerry and I have had terrible fights over it."

"I had no idea."

"I didn't want anyone to know about it," she said. "And I'm so embarrassed—please don't tell anyone, Syd."

I patted her leg and nodded. "You're not going to continue that, I hope."

She shook her head. "It's all been part of this crazy self-hatred I've felt. I've been trying to make myself into some kind of perfect woman, and—"

I waited for her to say *and it's stupid,* but she just shook her head. "I've been so depressed," she went on. "Nothing I could ever do was good enough. At least, that's what I thought. I would get up at three in the morning to work on scrapbooks."

"Seriously?"

She nodded. "I was trying to be Martha Stewart without a staff."

I laughed. "See? You're funny."

"That was my therapist's line."

"Oh."

"Anyway, do you know what finally made me crash?" She looked at me. "You getting pregnant again."

"What?" Okay, maybe my sister was certifiably nuts.

"I used to console myself that at least I had more kids than you did," she said. "And then when you got pregnant with your fifth, then we'd both have five."

Oh, my gosh. She was literally keeping score with number of children!

I had no idea what to say to this.

Donna looked ashamed and miserable. "I'm an idiot."

I rubbed her arm. "Yes, you are, honey."

Now she laughed. "You weren't supposed to agree with that."

I grinned. "Well, listen to yourself. Has your therapist said *that* yet? You sound like a lunatic, honey."

Donna laughed even harder.

"Listen," I said, getting serious. "You have always been the family valedictorian. You're the one who set the bar, Donna. You were the undisputed champion of everything you ever did. I didn't even *try* to compete because it was hopeless. You were six years older and there was no way to equal your accomplishments. I just stood back in awe along with the rest of the world."

She shook her head. "That's not how I saw it."

"Oh, great," I said. "So you're like these anorexic girls who look in the mirror, see skin and bones, and still think they're fat."

She nodded.

"Well, that's just nuts. You do need a therapist."

She smiled. "I know. But I've never felt I hit the finish mark, you know? When you're a perfectionist, that line keeps moving."

I thought for a moment. "Why can't you be an *im*perfectionist? That's what I do. The cake is crooked? Oh, well, it'll be fine. The lawn didn't get edged just right on one side? Oh, well, it'll be fine. Make that your motto: *It'll be fine.*"

"I even envied you for being able to do that," Donna said. "Syd, I've been depressed for years. Jerry put me on medication, but it didn't help. And then when I realized you were catching up to me with kids—"

A nurse came in to adjust Donna's beeping IV equipment then left again.

I sighed. "You poor thing," I said. How horrible to live such a tortured life, and for no good reason. It was pitiful. "I want to apologize for being the cause of your problems," I said, "but part of me thinks it's kind of crazy that you actually envied the little sister who could never do any of the exciting things you did. I can't even play the piano very well."

"Oh, I don't put the blame on you," Donna said. "My therapist says I have to own this and not blame anyone else."

Yay for the therapist; at least she isn't telling Donna it's all because of her mother.

"But you know what," Donna said, "a big part of this is because of Mom."

Oops, I spoke too soon.

"Really?" I said. "You're actually blaming Mom?"

"I'm not blaming her," Donna said. "But I do see how this whole perfectionism came from how we were raised. Nothing but the best was ever good enough."

"She does have a perfectionism streak," I said.

"Streak? STREAK?" Donna was almost shouting now. "Syd, it's an eight-lane highway!"

"Well . . ."

"Don't try to minimize it," Donna said. "Why do you think she always had us enter through the mudroom? I mean, did you ever once walk through our front door? She wanted all the dirt tracked in the back! That perfect front room was never even walked in!"

I tried to remember ever coming through the front door. No; we always came through the back door.

"And when I graduated from Primary and was invited to share an Article of Faith at the podium? I had to share *two* of them. All to please Mom. And that Pyrex dish she gave you?" Donna said. "Because it had tape burned on the end? She couldn't have an imperfect baking dish in her cupboard."

I could see Donna had a list of examples of how Mom had been too persnickety, too controlling. And I didn't want to sit and trash our mother, even if Donna was right.

"Look," I said. "I had lunch with her a while ago, and she realizes she made some mistakes there."

"She does?"

"We were talking about Ted. She really sees that she pushed too hard and didn't make him feel loved and accepted."

Donna was thunderstruck. "And she admitted this?"

"She brought it up."

Now Donna's jaw dropped. "Well, hallelujah. I mean, it's a bit late, but—"

"But at least she sees that she could have been less controlling," I said. "I think we need to give her credit for that."

Donna shrugged. "Okay. Anybody can see they did wrong. I mean, I am already seeing mistakes I'm making with my marriage and my kids."

I thought about Daniel. Maybe she'd lighten up on her demands and spare him the lifetime of rebellion Ted had lived.

"Well, just take it one step at a time," I said.

"That's what my therapist says."

"Hey," I joked, "look at the money I could save you. Pay *me* for advice instead. I'll charge half what the therapist charges."

"The first thing I'm going to do when I get home is gather the kids around and tell everybody why this happened and how I'm planning to change."

I could almost feel Daniel's load lightening.

"That doesn't mean we don't try to do our best, or that we slack off on doing right," she added, "but I'm going to be a lot less . . . fanatical."

I smiled. "Sounds like an excellent plan."

"And I'm going to post a sign on my bathroom mirror, listing my priorities. And if something I'm pushing for doesn't fit, I'm going to let it go."

"I like that," I said. "So how will your list read?"

"Testimony at the top," Donna said. "I mean, if the kids get scholarships and ribbons for all their other pursuits but they miss the most important goal, what have I accomplished?"

I smiled. This was exactly what Mom had said she regretted, and now Donna was breaking the chain and making her life Christ-centered.

"You are amazing," I said. "Do you know how many people ever get that right?"

"Are you going to give me a statistic?"

I laughed and leaned in to hug her. "I'm so proud of you."

Donna smirked. "But look what it took to wake me up."

"Hey, who cares? At least you got there," I said. "It's who you are right now that matters. What a great future you have ahead of you."

Donna's lunch arrived on a squeaky cart, and I stood up. "I'll let you eat your lunch," I said, "and get home to Cory and the kids."

"Thanks for everything," she said, "and for coming by."

"I love you," I said, and threw her a kiss.

She threw one back. "Me too."

I mulled over everything she had said as I drove home, and realized I need to back off as well—especially in trying to force Ted back into full activity. In many ways, I was a shadow of Donna. I didn't feel pressed to be perfect at everything, but I did try to micromanage other people's lives. Maybe it was me, not Ted, the Lord was waiting on.

That evening I got a ward email about a death in the stake, a woman I didn't know, but who had lived in our ward years earlier.

"Oh, look at this," I said. "A sister in the Third Ward passed away."

Ellie looked up from where she was playing with Juliet. "I guess somebody will be making funeral potatoes," she shrugged.

I nodded. "Yes, they will." Suddenly I felt a pang of interest, a wish that I could attend the funeral. Wait a minute: I hate funerals, right? So why do I want to attend the funeral of a woman I don't even know?

And then I realized how much I had learned at funerals during the last year. It hadn't been horrible at all; it had been inspiring. Real-life heroes had been honored, the gospel in its simple elegance had been summarized once again, and hearts had been touched. The Spirit had been there, and Ted had been there. It was my moment of hope for him—my hope that something said there would be his turning point.

I turned back to the computer and made a list—this time not of why funerals are terrible, but of what I had learned from them.

First, the death of a righteous person is not a thing of eternal consequence. Those sealed relationships continue, with but a brief physical separation.

Second, the key to getting along with others is to see them with loving parental eyes, the way God sees them. Reaching out to help them is vital.

Third, fault-finding is stupid. Okay, I need to reword that one to sound less blunt, but that's the absolute truth. Picking at flaws accomplishes nothing productive or useful and cheats you out of what could be a wonderful relationship with the person you're criticizing. You need to delve deeper into who they are and what makes them tick.

Fourth, enduring to the end doesn't just mean breathing and eating and getting by. It means being joyful and valiant and building the kingdom in every way you can, right until God sweeps you up into His arms again.

Fifth, life is hard by design. It's supposed to be. Fairness is a childish notion and a waste of time to pursue. The idea is to learn from whatever setbacks we encounter and not always kick and scream because we didn't get our way.

And last, we should be living right now the way we want to be remembered. If we want others to say we were kind, then we need to be known for that *now*. Tomorrow might never come.

I finished my list, pressed save, and realized I had six family home evening lessons all ready.

Donna was coming home tomorrow, Sunday, so everyone was gathering at my house for a delayed Thanksgiving dinner after church. I made pies and stuffing again, Mom was bringing her famous dinner rolls, Ted was bringing cranberry-orange relish, and the sisters-in-law were doing veggies and potatoes. I had a gigantic turkey ready to go into the oven at the crack of dawn, and the kids helped set the tables.

Chad and Neal had bumped their flights until Sunday night so they and their families could attend, and we all filled several benches at church Sunday morning. None of them had planned to stay past Saturday, so it was a comical flurry of clothing-borrowing to get all the kids and parents outfitted with dresses, shoes, white shirts, and ties.

But we did it, and everyone stumbled in, reasonably attired, while the prelude music was still playing.

Up on the stand I saw a guy about Ted's age talking to the bishop. Again my heart ached. If Ted would cut his hair and shave off his beard, I imagined he could look a lot like that man. It was all such a shame.

The man turned and came up the aisle toward where we were sitting. He could almost be Ted's twin. He got closer then stopped at our bench. I looked at him then looked again. I gasped. It *was* Ted!

"Ted!" I exclaimed. "What are you doing here?"

"Well, that's a fine how-do-you-do." He laughed. Then he squeezed in and sat between me and Hayden.

My eyes must have looked like dinner plates, because Ted laughed again and rubbed my back. "I figured maybe I'd start coming to church again," he said. "It's not my home ward, but I thought I'd come here first."

"What?!" Tears were tumbling from my eyes, fat droplets landing on my blue blouse.

Ted squeezed my shoulders.

"And you shaved!" I gasped, suddenly realizing his beard was gone. "You must be serious."

"I am." He smiled.

"How . . . how . . . why . . ." I stammered.

He looked around then whispered in my ear. "It was Daniel," he said. "I went over to Donna's last night to talk to him, and I could see my life stretching out before me all over again. I realized I was acting just like him, and felt like a big ol' dope. I thought, *How can I help this kid when I'm doing exactly the same thing?*"

I was stunned. All my scheming, all my begging—and it was a nephew's rebellion that did it.

"I knew the Church was true," he whispered. "I just wanted to prove that I couldn't be bossed around. Pretty stupid, huh?"

I was still just staring at him and crying joyful tears.

"You were right about that," he said. "If I'm rebelling against Mom and Dad, then they still have all the power. Who was I kidding?"

"Shh!" It was Ellie, enforcing the rules of reverence in the chapel.

"I'm so happy," I said, finally able to speak a full sentence.

"Me too," he said. "High time."

I couldn't stop crying, and I waved my fingertips at my eyes.

Ted whispered again. "Why do women always fan their eyes when they cry?"

"Only 65 percent of us do," I said.

"Oh, another thing," Ted said. "Funeral potatoes."

"Huh?"

"It's our culture." He grinned. "Every time you made them, it reminded me of who we are. Who I am. I'm a Mormon guy, plain and simple."

I leaned my head on his shoulder.

Ted turned his head slightly. "You're not crying on my new suit, I hope."

I laughed. This was going to be the best Thanksgiving ever.

Chapter 21

AND, EXCEPT FOR PEANUT SNATCHING a drumstick from one of the young nephews and running through the house like a greased pig no one could catch, it was a wonderful feast. More than that, it was a celebration. We were thrilled at Donna's return and her ability to face her demons, admit them, and set a new course. More than anything, we were glad she didn't seem to be permanently damaged and unable to climb out again, as Jerry had so feared.

Except for Daniel, the kids seemed ready and willing to get back to normal family life but with a much less wound-up mother. Daniel was still aloof, unwilling to forgive the terrible childhood he felt he'd had. His resentment went deep, and he seemed determined to lick his wounds and blame his mother for every hurt he'd ever felt.

And our other celebration was, of course, that Ted was coming back into the fold. "Heck, I can't even spell *prodigal*; I figured I ought to stop being one," he joked.

And then, halfway through dinner, before we had even gotten to our alphabetical gratitude list, Mom surprised us with a heartfelt apology for her part in both their situations.

"I know you'll all say not to blame myself and that everyone can make their own choices," she began, "but I'd like both Ted and Donna to know how truly sorry I am that I pushed so hard."

Everyone erupted into a flurry of *no you didn't* and *it wasn't your fault,* probably just to get over the awkwardness of such an emotional moment. But Mom waved it away and kept going. "I did," she insisted. "I've thought long and hard about my mistakes as a mother, and I want you kids to know I love you both without condition."

"Hey, what about me?" I said, trying to lighten up the seriousness.

She smiled. "I love you all," she said. "But I think my relentlessness took a particular toll on Ted and Donna. I would do it all so differently." She began to cry; Dad squeezed her shoulders and stroked her cheek.

"You were a wonderful mother," he said.

We all agreed, but Mom wasn't finished. "I was badly mistaken many a time," she said. "And I hope you can all learn from my mistakes. Love others exactly as they are," she said. "Let your kids be the people they were born to be, not some manufactured image of your own making."

I stole a glance at Daniel, whose face visibly softened and who was staring straight at Donna. I looked at Donna, and she was smiling at her son through tumbling tears.

"You did so many things right," I said, uncomfortable with Mom's complete *mea culpa*. "You're the woman we all admire most."

Everyone agreed, but Mom still wasn't finished. "I'm just grateful things have all worked out," she said. "And it's not because of me; it's because of you kids, yourselves. I'm proud of every one of you."

"To the OllerVanKeefer Wunder Kids," I said, raising my water glass in a toast. "We really are something."

Everyone laughed, but Mom tapped her glass again for attention. "I'm not finished," she said. And for the first time I saw how tiny and frail she was, how thin her voice had become, how diminished she was from the powerhouse I remembered as a little girl.

"I want to invite all of you over tomorrow night for pizza."

Now there was confused silence. We weren't sure if she was losing her marbles or what.

"I want you to track mud through the front door," she said, "and we're going to eat the pizza in the living room."

"On the sofa?" Chad asked, voicing all of our shock.

"On the sofa, on the chairs, on the carpet—wherever you want!" Mom beamed. "High time, I say."

Dad was smiling, his eyes brimming with happy tears as he watched his bride take such a huge step.

Somebody whistled, somebody hooted, and within seconds we were all cheering. I had thought we were celebrating Donna and Ted, but it turned out Mom was the big surprise, the one who had caught us most off guard.

"Wow," I said to Cory as we were clearing dishes an hour later. "Can you believe Mom?"

"She's amazing," he agreed. "What an example of how you can always change and grow, at any age."

"I'm still kind of . . . astounded," I said. "To admit you've done something wrong. That is so, well, not my mother."

"Turns out it *is* your mother. She's taken a stride none of us expected."

"I admire her so much more now," I said. "We're finally open and honest, you know? I mean, that never flew in our family before. We had to hide our flaws. But this—this feels so . . ." I searched for the word. *"Free."*

Neal came in just then and overheard me. "It's liberating, isn't it? I had no idea how stifled we all were until now."

I looked at him, somewhat surprised. Neal had felt stifled?

"I mean, even being able to admit to little things," he said. "I never felt I could do that. One time I broke a mug, and I wrapped it up in a garbage bag and threw it away rather than admit I had broken something. Crazy!"

I smiled. Somehow it triggered a memory of mine, of leaving my blankets wrinkled under a puffy new comforter I got when I was twelve. All day at school I agonized over not making my bed correctly, worrying that somehow I'd be found out, that my sloppiness would be discovered. Crazy indeed.

Chad and his wife joined us, carrying in serving dishes. "This is really making me take a second look at how I'm raising my kids," Chad said. "Everyone repeats mistakes, but if we look at it consciously instead of just following old habits, that's a good thing."

"Hallelujah," his wife whispered, grinning.

"You watch," Chad told her. "You're going home with a different man." She raised her eyebrows and laughed. "Seriously," he said. "I'm going to lighten up and be a lot less demanding."

Somehow the rest of the family ended up in the kitchen and, as if we were suddenly in a giant support group, we started sharing our new outlook and new ideas about how to raise kids without such a heavy load of guilt.

I noticed Ted wasn't there and glanced out the side window to a driveway where Cory had installed a basketball hoop a couple of years ago. Ted and Daniel were shooting hoops and I saw them high-five.

"Look," I said. "Ted and Daniel."

Everyone followed my gaze and watched as the two of them played, Daniel dribbling around Ted's block and taking a shot that sank smoothly through the net.

"I thought Ted hated ball sports," Chad whispered to me.

"He does," I said, "but he loves Daniel."

Chad smiled. "He's always been the best uncle. Talk about hitting the 'perfect' mark without even trying."

It was true. Daniel was in good hands. And, finally, so was Ted.

Book Club Questions

1. What's your impression of Syd? Does she remind you of anyone you know? What are her strengths? Her weaknesses?
2. Do you or anyone here have a hard time relaxing?
3. Do you know any families who are high achievers? Are there any rebels in the mix?
4. How do we measure success? Are we still looking at income and worldly achievements? How can we correct that?
5. What makes one child in a family fight against and resist authority, while others are more compliant?
6. Syd tells Ted that when he makes choices in reaction to his parents' wishes, he's still giving them all the power. Is this true?
7. Syd comes from a family that has placed an inordinate amount of focus on appearances. How is this a mistaken pursuit?
8. How honest and open should we be with our children? Do we hide certain facts about relatives—or ourselves—in order to present a proper example? Is this a good idea, or not?
9. Do you struggle with perfectionism? How does such a struggle impact children? Have you conquered it? If so, how?
10. Have you ever felt your problems outweigh another person's, perhaps someone whom everyone rallies to help, while you struggle silently? How do you get back on track from self-pity?
11. Is competition healthy, or is it rooted in jealousy and resentment, as Syd claims?
12. Is it true that "nothing of eternal consequence has happened here" when someone dies in full fellowship, active in Church service?

13. How far can you go in trying to reactivate a loved one? What can you pray for, and what actions can you personally take?
14. How do you find ways to reach outside your circle of LDS friends and get involved in the community, as Ruby Barnes did?
15. Have you ever tried to be a match-maker with disastrous results? What did you learn from the experience?
16. What do you think about women having secret charge accounts?
17. Does anyone here identify with Syd in being unable to play the piano or in having terrible hand-to-eye coordination? Do you have any children like this?
18. Have you taken an aptitude test? What did it advise, and have you actually pursued that advice?
19. What do you think of Syd's list of advice for newlyweds? What would you add to that list?
20. How do you feel about funerals? How would you change them?
21. Have you ever had a relative who has fallen away from the Church, for whom you've fasted and prayed? Are you still waiting for that person to return to activity? If so, how do you find peace and patience?
22. Have you ever wondered what will be said at your funeral? How would you like to be remembered, and how can you change your behavior to be that way today?

About the Author

Joni Hilton has written several award-winning plays, seventeen books, and dozens of magazine articles. She holds a master of fine arts degree in professional writing from USC and frequently contributes to MeridianMagazine.com. She also writes for "Music and the Spoken Word."

Sister Hilton is currently serving as Relief Society president in her ward in northern California and has previously served as a regional media specialist for Public Affairs, first counselor in a stake Relief Society, Relief Society president and counselor, seminary teacher, Gospel Doctrine teacher, and has worked in the Primary and Young Women organizations.

Joni is a former TV talk show host, radio host, and Miss California. She continues to tour the United States as a corporate spokeswoman on TV. She is also a busy motivational speaker and the founder and former CEO of an organic line of cleaning products. Sister Hilton is an avid cook and has won more than sixty cook-offs and recipe contests. She is married to Bob Hilton and is the mother of four children. You can learn more on her website at www.jonihilton.com.